The first indication they had arrived w
glinting coming from the car park as vehicle
after vehicle crept down the hill to claim an £18
for 4 hours space. The sound of Sleepwalk by
the Shadows played languidly from the
sandwich bar by the ticket machine.

All those camper vans and all-terrain vehicles
competing for spaces which were so snug it
was hard to get a motorcycle into some of
them.

Of course if you come to Cornwall , you do
actually need a machine which is a hybrid of an
arctic ice breaker and a deep dessert assault
vehicle. It's well known that the terrain is
extreme. The absence of duel carriageways for
instance or the complex survival issues of not
having a Macdonald or Costa dotted every ¼
mile present massive challenges for which
visitors must be prepared!

Denzel Sprygelly gazed over the car-park from
his balcony and rubbed his hands with glee. It
was going to be a profitable weekend. Denzel
was from the proper old school of Cornish
businessmen and it didn't matter to him what

the law was regarding minimum wage. His staff were getting £3 and hour and no breaks, like it or lump it. He allowed himself a little chuckle.

Accent's from across the Tamar floated over the river adding their own distinct notes to the symphony of Emmet sound.
"Beep beep! Honk! squeal of tyres, 'you bleedy idiot!' The sound of a taxi screeching to a halt as people stepped into the road preferring to cross 20 meters from the pedestrian crossing rather than at the crossing itself.
" Harrrrrlow! Get here now!" "Ocean , River, no babes, we'll git you an oice cream in a min-nut"

A Range Rover on steroids stopped in the middle of the main access to the town with no regard for other road users and hailed what appeared to be a bona fida resident from the pavement.

"Ere mate. Do you know the way to Polperro?" "Yes thanks" the man replied, and walked off.

Newly arrived Damien nudged Channella and gestured a sign as they passed a pub. "Look babes, they got the footie on this afternoon"

"Oh great" she answered, " look, Stella is only £6.80 a pint, bargain! I fink I might try that Rattler though, look at that, it's only £5.50, whys it got a snake on the picture? "
Clearly the overnight drive of 300 miles to sit and watch football in a boozer had been worth it.

Just a short distance away from where Damien and Channella admired the beer prices, another adventure was beginning to unfold. Hot, tired and agitated from their long journey, Troy and Leafetta had finally arrived at their holiday apartment. It had been a difficult journey. No one had told them there would be tractors on the road during their 24 mile trip from Plymouth. Troy had already drunk almost their entire supply of Red Bull.

They hadn't realised it might be important to bring the directions to their holiday apartment in the car with them. Looe was only a small place they thought so it ought to be easy enough to find Emmety Villa just by looking? They had no idea there were so many roads in the town, they'd thought it was just a high street and a beach, a bit like at the theme parks. They'd been astonished to discover that people actually lived here. It was all very confusing and stupid!

There was one good thing which had occurred though. Just as they'd left Saltash, the exhaust on their prized Vauxhall Corse has begun to pull apart. Now it was rumbling gratifyingly just like the one's Troy's mates had to 'burn up the Hoe' on a Friday night. All Troy needed now to feel complete was turbo, and another six tattoos.

Leafetta had other thoughts on her mind, it was a special anniversary. She and Troy had been together for almost three weeks now and she was determined that the time was right to have a baby.

She was wearing the brand new peach leggings she'd had to get on special order from Primark. For some reason all the ones she liked seem to sell out really quickly, so she'd had to reserve hers from the next delivery. It had been an anxious wait, but worth it. She knew that as she walked down the street, people would think she was naked. Leafetta loved it when the men ogled her. She'd made sure her tee shirt was short enough to clearly show off her beloved 'Green Army' tattoo which beamed frenzy of Celtic knot work just over the top of her pelvis, where her fruttock pulled the skin tight enough to read it.

As they dragged their cases up the 120 steps to their apartment, their thoughts turned to food. They hadn't eaten since breakfast time and although the Burger King special should have set them up for the day, they were craving some traditional seaside food. On one of their many circuits around the one way system they seen both a kebab shop and a pizza restaurant, so they knew that once they'd offloaded their luggage, all their needs would be met.

From behind the blinds of his apartment, Maurice watched as Troy and Leafetta headed down the steps of Emmety Villa and presumably, into the town.

Maurice had lived in the town for almost three years now, so technically, he was still a 'blow in', in another twenty two years he'd be considered a local though, so he did his absolute best to emulate what he felt we expected of him.

"Bloody Emmets!" he muttered to himself, and then "No dammit! , try again! Bleedy Emmets!, that's better"

He wondered how long the holiday apartments would be let for this time? Probably just the weekend, but if not, he'd do his best to make them feel unwelcome anyway. The more crappy reviews the apartments got on trip advisor he thought, the less likely people were to book it.

He scowled, bloody emmets coming here and spoiling the place!

Now the couple had gone, he went to his porch and grabbed the special tool for turning the stopcock and a screwdriver. He deftly flicked open the cast steel cover by the main door and gave the stop cock for the holiday apartment two swift turns before closing the cover again and retreating back to his lair.

Maurice enjoyed his little game. Every time

someone new arrived he would turn the stop cock of the holiday apartment down so that barely a trickle of water ran through the taps. Sometimes the visitors would knock on his door and ask if his water was off, sometimes they would go straight ahead and ring the letting agency. Then the agency would ring Maurice to ask if his water was off.

Maurice knew it generally took the agencies maintenance man Simon, several hours to get to his building. Simons main job kept him occupied until at least 5pm. By then, Maurice would have opened the stop cock again, only to nip out and turn it down again once the confused Simon had found absolutely nothing wrong and gone home. Simon would get his call-out fee and as Maurice was always so helpful and offered him coffee when he visited, Simon always bought Maurice a pint when he saw him in the pub.

Maurice wondered whether the other holiday apartment in loft of the building would have visitors this week, probably he reasoned, it was 'that time of year' after all.

At least the people who came to the other apartment were easier to live with. The owner had made sure the place was thoroughly insulated and thus relatively soundproof. Maurice hated having to listen to the bloody emmet s when they clumped around the holiday lets, people were so inconsiderate. He picked up his bagpipes and began to practise Amazing Grace. He would leave piano practise until tomorrow. He had a busy evening planned.

River and Ocean had won. Channella was mentally exhausted, not from the exploits with the children, unfortunately she'd been born like it.

She fiddled constantly with her tongue stud trying to find answers to life's big questions. Where were the loos? Would she be able to watch EastEnders tonight? Where was the nearest branch of Matalan?

From a window somewhere over their heads, 'Tequila!' Was being played on a loop and drifted across the town forming a soundtrack for the visitors perform to.

Damien hovered outside the Ice cream shop smoking a roll up and gazing lustily at the baseball caps being modelled in the window of the adjacent shop. He was particularly amused with one which read 'I caught crabs in Looe'. That's nothing he thought, he'd caught crabs in Grantham *and* Spalding. He'd caught something a lot more serious in Lincoln last weekend but now wasn't the time to tell Channella. As far as she was concerned, he'd gone to watch the match.

River and Ocean pressed their faces into the glass front of the large display cabinet leaving snotty smears. They asked the poor girl behind the counter to tell them all forty flavours for the third time.

Bethany sighed and patiently ran through the list again. She knew it was pointless. In the end both little girls would choose the bubble-gum flavoured blue one which would then be promptly discarded in the nearest bin.

She looked at the queue as people shuffled and tutted impatiently.
As Bethany ran through the list robot fashion, her mind wandered.

Why was there a bare chested fat sweaty bloke with a Man United tattoo on his breast almost every single day?
How many of them were there in the world?
Quite a few from what she'd witnessed.
Did they all have 4 ice creams a day?
Why did they turn up in the pub later in the day after work, and then ooze up to her and pretend they were old friends?

Bethany allowed herself a small shudder. She'd have gone and worked in the other big ice cream shop or one of the arcades if she could. Uncle Denzel wouldn't like that though, and Uncle Denzel was on every committee in town. Uncle Denzel, or as he was known when wore his apron, Brother Denzel, could make life either difficult, or impossible, there was no alternative.

"We want that one". screamed both little girls pointing at the predicted tub of blue nastiness. God knows what horrors it contained. Luckily hardly anyone ever managed to finish eating a whole one.

Now came the decision which of the 12 choices

of cone the girls would have.
Bethany felt another tiny piece of her soul slip
away into a void of despair and
meaninglessness.
Maurice put down his bagpipes and decided it
was time to move to phase two. He took his
spare keys from the kitchen drawer and
stepped outside heading for the compost heap
at the end of the garden.

Maurice had keys for three of the six
apartments now. Those key code boxes took a
little patience to get open at first, but he'd found
a helpful burglars trick on You- tube and now
he could open one in less than three minutes.

On reaching the compost heap, to his delight,
he looked down to see a fresh writhing of
maggots inside the pile of mince he'd left out
specifically for that purpose.
Maurice was getting as good at maggots as he
was at stealing keys. These would be the bright
green flies he reckoned, perfect!

He tipped the maggots into a sandwich bag and
then let himself into the apartment next to his
own.

He was surprised to see a pile of luggage. He'd thought the young couple he'd seen earlier were travelling light. The more luggage they had, generally, the longer they stayed. He groaned inwardly and then groaned again. The ones who arrived later generally had offspring. Maurice loathed children even more than he loathed bloody emmet s, and that was a lot of loathing. Oh well, at least the water was already done he consoled himself.

The first job was always to reach behind the cooker and turn off the tap which controlled the gas supply.
When the owners rang their 'helpful neighbour' to ask him to have a quick look, he always blamed the cleaners. The owners of the lower flat had gone through at least eight different cleaners so far this season. Upstairs was on the fourth but Maurice was working on that. The owners would get fed up soon Maurice reasoned, then with a bit of luck they'd stop letting the bloody, 'bleddy' he corrected himself, place out.

Troy and Leafetta had brought so much

luggage it looked as if they were going to stay all summer.

Maurice eyed up the pink suitcases but stopped himself from investigating any further. He could get himself some of Leafettas ample knickers when the couple went out tomorrow, once they'd been worn.

That wasn't a day one task he reminded himself, now back to the job at hand.

The cleaners had done a great job he noticed as he sprinkled maggots down the back of the fridge. Not a wisp of dust remained under the bed he observed as he put more maggots on the floor below the stained mattress. A few more behind the bath panel and he was done. Now back to the compost heap and then up to repeat the procedure in what was laughingly called Emmety Villa Penthouse.

Maurice worked diligently, but just as he was about to exit the apartment, he heard footsteps on the stairs. He sighed in relief as they stopped by number five and a door closed behind either Alan, the chap who lived there, or Eileen, his wife.

Apparently they were both cousins of Denzel Sprygelly, Maurice was still trying to work that one out.

It would be pub time soon, he'd relax with a nice pint for a while. This in reality meant he'd sit for three hours at the bar with a single pint which he'd scowl over the top of at anyone he didn't know.
He was in good company, in the Grumpy Seafarer, that's what all the locals did.
Maurice liked the landlord at the Grumpy.
Apparently, he was one of Denzel's cousins.

Leafetta screamed loudly as a gull swooped down and took her second pasty right out of her hand. "That was close" she said and took a long drag on the cigarette she'd been smoking. For a few seconds Troy laughed uproariously, spitting pieces of swede and pastry all over the pavement. Troy's laugh was reminiscent of a hyena caught in snake pit. He stopped abruptly when a second gull swooped from behind and deftly removed his pasty from his grip too.
There , in full view of everyone else on the seafront, he proceeded to throw a tantrum.
A different gull hopped close to his foot trying to

grab some of the crumbs. Troy lashed out with his trainered foot. Fortunately, he missed the gull entirely. Unfortunately, he didn't miss Michael Sprygelly who happened to be passing at the time.
At 6'8 and 22stone, Michael was hard to miss anywhere.

He gasped for breath as his testicles rushed towards his oesophagus. Despite the excruciating pain, Michael locked eyes with the now petrified Troy as only a true Cornish rugby player can. Troy could run, but Michael would remember his face until his last breath. Michael mewed like a kitten and collapsed onto the paving clutching his essentials.

Leafetta has the presence of mind to grab Troy's arm, and as quickly as they could, they waddled away from the distraught, now weeping figure on the concrete.

Leafetta took the lead. "Oh blinkin 'eck! I need another pasty now. Shall we go back to that coffee place or do you want to try the bakery on the other side?"
Troy stood beside her in a flood of adrenaline,

not really understanding what she was saying and then over her shoulder he spotted something which immediately brought him back to his senses. He had spotted the amusement arcade.

Just a short distance away, River was vomiting in a shop doorway for all her worth. Fluorescent blue liquid spilled out of her splattering over the buckets and spades and crab nets. It was all too much for Ocean, who decided that she would join in too.

The Tardis like qualities of children really come to the fore where ice cream is involved. About an eighth of a pint goes in, and almost a full gallon comes back out again. Try doing that when you grow up!

Channella dabbed at the faces of the distressed girls with a wet wipe and ignored the frosty gaze coming from the owner of the shop.

"I'll get you a bucket so you can clean that up" he offered.

Channella ignored him and waited for Ocean to finish so she could finish dabbing. She drew another wet wipe from the packet and dropped the most recently used one onto the floor of the doorway to join a growing collection.

Taking a daughter in each hand she gathered her children towards her and announced to the world in general. "Come on giwls, let's take our custom to a nicer shop"
The whole pantomime from their arrival to their departure had taken a full five minutes, it would take considerably longer to clear up.

The shop owner, a cousin of Denzel's, shook his head in dismay and asked one of his girls to watch the till whilst he cleaned up the mess. Undoubtedly this wouldn't be the last time this season but at least he had some decent footage for Sunday's pub viewing.

You'm a celebrity! the programme was called. Every Saturday evening, former BBC producer and local hotelier Noel Hopkins, a cousin of Denzel's, would edit together all the snippets from the week.

Shop lifters, dog poo leavers, pewkers and litter louts all featured in what regularly ran to a full 30 minutes of footage. The completed programme was then uploaded to You-tube and played to audiences at two hour intervals in all the pubs and restaurants in the town for a week.

It had proved incredibly popular, not to mention lucrative. It was often said that the good people of Looe had a few funny ideas. They were absolutely brilliant when it came to making people famous.

She didn't know it yet, but Channella had arrived!

She hurried the two simpering girls along the street wondering where Damien might have gotten to. Outside a pub was a sign which read "Drink 9 pints of Stella, have a 10th on us for free"
The place was packed and a mixture of Midlands, Welsh and Yorkshire accents which floated out onto the street.
This had to be the place.
As she ventured through the crowded bar, other accents became audible, over here a Mancunian, and sitting with her a Londoner. A whole symphony of voices including virtually

every accent of the nation, except Cornish.

Channella spotted Damien leaning against the bar and headed towards him.
"Did you get me one babes?" she asked.
"Oh sorry luv" he answered " I got two pints but you were so long I'm just finishing yours, I'll get some more. Giwls?"

He looked at the upturned faces still plastered in blue, he didn't seem to notice their tee shirts were plastered too.
"Here you go, I got you fruits shoots, do you want crisps?"
"I want coke daddy!" River demanded.

Half a dozen blokes paused their glasses en route to their mouths as for a horrified minute they all assumed they had been found by their own children.
"And I want Fanta!" Ocean swiftly added.

The relieved drinkers resumed.

Never underestimate how much crap a small child on holiday can ingest over the course of a day.

Of course it will probably re-emerge in a variety of ways, buy hey, they're just kids, they deserve a few treats.

Sunrising estate was generally peaceful, well-kept and trouble free. Holiday makers did not venture into this part of Looe much. The walkers usually confined themselves to the cliff paths. There were only a couple of holiday lets here ,so Sunrising tended to escape the disruption which holiday makers brought with them.

There was no doubt that the residents enjoyed a party or barbecue as much as any visitor, but these tended to be confined to weekends . In nearby Millendreath, of the 176 Villas dotted along the hillside, only 1 in 15 was a residence these days. The visitors just wanted to enjoy themselves, everyone understood that. For anyone such as the local postie though, people partying next door four or five nights on the trot became a little intrusive, especially if the party was still going just half an hour before he had to go to work. Sleep deprived neighbours don't make for welcoming locals.

Sunrising was different though, and until recently, it had been unusual to see a police car here.

P.C. Veryan Bolitho, one of Denzel Sprygellys cousins, closed her notebook, thanked her cousin Julie for the tea, and walked back to the patrol car. There had been at least a dozen similar incidents like this over the previous two months, which made Veryan suspicious that this was crime was being committed by someone who lived in the area.

Sitting in the driver's seat she radioed through to her Sargent.

"You were right" She said "Our frilly felon has been at it again" Sargent Lowenna Bolitho, Denzel's cousin, responded with a knowing "Hmmm" "Did anyone spot our naughty knickers nicker this time? "

"No I'm afraid our panty pervert is as elusive as ever"

"What about evidence? Did our lacy lingerie line

lightener leave any footprints?”

“As far as I can see our Briefs and Brazier Burglar hasn't left a trace” Veryan replied

“I detest these sleazy stocking stealer's” Lowenna responded “Why can't they just order on line from Marks like the other weirdos?”

“Have we had a G-string Jockey in Looe before then?” Veryan asked.

“We have” Lowenna answered with a sigh “Although he was more of a covert corset coveter than a secret skivvies snatcher”

“I'm at a complete loss then” Veryan paused “And it's as if he knows where all the CCTV is in town too. Not one theft has been on any of the cameras”

“I'm sure he'll come skidding to an abrupt halt when he does” the Sargent answered before adding “That is of course assuming it's a bloke?” She just as quickly dismissed the idea “Not that that's likely “ She continued “Most of the weirdos around here are on a committee or club, and we know full well they don't let women join"

Veryan agreed. "While I've got you Sarge? Our Julie asked if you're coming to Nana's party on Sunday? "

"I'm not on duty so I guess, as usual, it just depends how long it takes to process all the Saturday night numpties. You haven't forgotten we're busy tonight?"

"No I haven't, but hopefully we'll be done before Mike finishes"

Veryan signed off the radio. What she needed was someone who knew all about the goings on in town. She smiled as she thought of just the person. Her cousin Gale of course. Gale, Denzel's niece twice removed, ran the fish and chip shop on the fish quay, and there wasn't a single piece of important gossip she didn't know about.

Maurice watched the police car pull away. He was feeling cheated. He'd been eyeing up that particular line for weeks now, and dammit! He almost stamped his foot; his rival had beaten him to it again. He continued his walk around the estate and planned his route. He'd be back later

Troy was completely riveted to the flashing lights and spinning wheels of his chosen machine. Another few spins and he'd have £5.00 in the 'bank'. He loaded a few more pound coins into the slot. He realised that he'd almost run out of the 40 he'd gotten from the change booth on the way in, but that didn't matter, he was winning!

Leafetta held her breath as she dropped another 50 pence into the slot on the coin pusher.
A little girl beside her bent down to pick her dolly up from the floor. For a second from her stooped perspective, she gazed at the mound of coins inside the machine. On standing back up again she announced to the world in general. "No wonder I couldn't win. It's all stuck down with blue tack"
Denzel had clearly discovered a winning formula. The local council gaming officer was a

cousin of Denzel's, and a case of Rattler every Christmas ensured that the blue tack was never discussed.

In the Galleon, Damien and Channella were enjoying their fifth and seventh pints. They'd have to go soon thought Damien. He'd left the 4x4 in the main car park and the website had said they could get into Emmety Villa Penthouse after 3pm.
He'd be fine to drive he reckoned, anyway, he was a good driver. He'd have had a pasty by then, and there was no point in missing out on a free pint.

It was going to be a great holiday he thought. Channella didn't know about his rash yet and the cream he'd gotten from the clinic appeared to be working which was a bonus.
He'd worked hard for a week to get money for this holiday, ferrying his drug dealer mates around the fens. For a minute he felt sad as he remembered the day the police had confiscated his Subaru from him, he'd loved that car.

He glanced towards the bar where Channella was navigating her way through the crowd with more Stella for them both, and some more pop and crisps for the giwls.

Yes it was going to be great. The kids could play on the beach. He and Channella could drink blackcurrant cider in the sun all day, and if he were really lucky, he might even start a fight. Not that attacking someone from behind was technically a fight, but it still made him feel very tough.
If it looked like he was in any real danger, he knew Channella would wade in and save him. "My little Bulldog" he would call her affectionately, and in truth, her resemblance to one was stunning.

"Where are the giwls?" He asked as Channella sloshed the fresh drinks all over the tray and table.
"I sent them to play in that toy shop next door" she answered "They must be happy, they've been gone nearly an hour."

In the shop next door, Veryan had arrived.

River and Ocean had managed to destroy around £400 worth of stock even before the shopkeeper had called the control room. He'd tried to intervene only for the six and seven-year-olds to scream 'PERVERT' and "LEAVE US ALONE!" at the tops of their voices. They knew exactly how to play this game, that's why there was an injunction forbidding them entry to every shop in Sleaford.

All the other customers had fled.

Veryan observed the carnage as she approached the girls. Torn display boxes and abandoned and broken toys littered the entire floor. River was offering one of the supersize teddies a sip of her Fanta, pouring the sticky liquid all over it. The shop keeper mentally added another £250 to the insurance claim.

Veryan knew there was almost nothing she could do. The chances of actually gaining a prosecution for most of the incidents she dealt with were rare. If it was locals she had to deal with, outcomes of police intervention depended on who was related to whom and to which special club they belonged.

She approached the girls slowly having already

guessed where the parents were.

Rude though it clearly was, a lot of people seemed to think it was just fine to send their children into shops unsupervised to entertain themselves. The parents never took responsibility for the subsequent damage.

It was also astonishing that some of these children made their way safely back to their parents. A busy town like Looe attracted every sort of pervert, weirdo and predator. Veryan had worked on cases where the children hadn't been found until it was too late to save them. Scenes like this made her quite cross. Nevertheless, she dealt with it with complete professionalism.

Smiling at the girls who had now noticed her, she moved her gaze from Ocean to River and then back again before gently saying "Hello girls, what are your names?"

Ocean was in her feet in a thrice, she darted for the door of the shop. River knew how to react too. As Veryan's gaze was averted, impressed by the speed of Oceans departure, River dashed around a fitting and also exited the premises.

She might have only been six, but she was fast,

fast enough to grab the Barbie she'd hidden in a pile of sandcastle buckets in the doorway. She wasn't going to let that one go.

By the time Veryan had made it to the doorway, both girls were back in the bar and already hurriedly sitting down. Veryan knew there was no point in pursuit. Even though the on-street CCTV would show exactly where the girls had gone, she knew both they and their parents would say they'd been in the pub the entire time.

Veryan shock her head. The shop owner was a cousin so undoubtedly there would be more tea while she dealt with the aftermath with him.

She wondered how many other similar incidents she'd have today. Oh well, she thought, just another normal day at the office.

Troy and Leafetta left the the arcade clutching their prizes. Troy had claimed his fiver and Leafetta was very proud of the foot-high plastic monkey she'd just won. £80 lighter than when they'd gone in, they were happy. They'd accomplished something. It was almost quarter to twelve now so they'd just have time for a pasty or few doughnuts before lunch at 1pm.

Troy scanned the street in case that giant he'd had his accident with earlier was anywhere to be seen. He was relieved to discover he wasn't. He tried to relax a little, it was difficult though. Leaving the familiar streets of Plymouth brought all sorts of potential hazards. Troy preferred the safety and anonymity the city offered. He and the rest of his crew were true Plymouth Brethren. Troy missed his mates. Normally by this time on a Saturday he'd be sleeping off his regular Friday night antics, and a bottle of Southern Comfort.

As they headed down the street, Troy noticed two blue stained little girls tear out of a shop doorway and immediately disappear into the pub next door. He flinched reflexively when the girls were swiftly followed onto the street by a uniformed WPC. He paused and pulling his hoodie a little tighter, pretended to be busy looking through the window of a fishing tackle shop.
Veryan stepped back inside the shop and Troy reminded himself quietly that no one here knew

him.

Leafetta had spotted the advert for the free pint of Stella. "I think I found our new local" she said "Still, it's a shame they haven't got a 'Spoons yet. I thought every town had to have one? "

Troy smiled lustfully at her. She was a great girl. She didn't mind sharing dog end roll ups with him and in the three weeks they'd been together, she hadn't once suggested he try some fresher underpants or wash his grey flannel joggers. She hadn't minded when he'd forgotten to take the tag off the flowers he'd given her either.
"We'll miss you Aunty Beryl , Rest in peace, love always from Noah and Julius" it had read.

She could drink like a fish too, and she was great at either lifting other people's pints, or getting other people to pay for theirs.
"We're celebrating because we both just got jobs at Wrigleys" She'd tell the other guidable boozers. "Next Friday we're going to come back here and then the drinks are definitely on us all night! " She'd say.
The fools would be falling over themselves to

buy the pair a half each. It might only come a pint at a time, but it worked like a charm. On a good afternoon over a couple of pubs, Troy and Leafetta could average at least a gallon and a half each. So far they'd worked their way around most of the pubs in Crownhill. They were off to try Mutley when they went home.

Leafetta was speaking to him so he brought his attention back to the moment
"........or shall we have a Chinese?" she was asking.

As he walked through town, Maurice recognised the large girl in the skin colour leggings and her anaemic looking hoodied cohort.
He chuckled as he remembered the unloading scene back at Emmety Villa earlier in the morning.
He'd almost given himself a hernia laughing as the couple had sweated and sworn while dragging their luggage up the steps.
He'd noticed the Green Army sticker on their Corsa as he'd left home for his morning walk too.
"Oh" he'd muttered to himself "Janners!"

Maurice knew that there were two distinctly different types of Janners. There were the really kind, friendly, generous, warm hearted, give you their last pound type. He'd met a few of them here on day trips, lovely people.

Then there was the other sort, and these two he decided, fitted into that category. He'd better make sure his windows and shed were properly locked.
Quite ironic really for a man who let himself into other people's flats and regularly stole underwear from his neighbours washing lines.

Maurice continued on his daily stomp down to the seafront. He wondered if his friend Tony was working today. Tony looked after the seafront; nice bloke was Tony. Peculiarly for the town, Tony wasn't related to Denzel Spygelly in any way at all.
Of course he had to have dealings with him, there was hardly anyone in town who didn't. Tony wasn't like the rest of them though, he wasn't prepared to compromise his integrity. Maurice wasn't sure he approved of that, but he thought of Tony as a mate.

Maurice made sure he left Tony's washing line alone. Integrity wasn't always visible, but in Tony's case it clearly was. If Maurice ever spotted the other knickers nicker anywhere near Tony's place, he'd be straight on the phone to Veryan or Lowenna. He even had their personal numbers if it came to that, after all, they were friends too, so he thought.

"....and the fing is" Maurice persisted "They use all the flippin toilet roll and then wash the sand off their feet in the blinkin sinks"

Tony was doing his best to be polite but really, another rant from Maurice was the last thing on his mind right now. Tony had been on the beach since 5am picking up used nappies and discarded lager cans. The toilets were nothing to do with him. He'd had to remove another dead dolphin from the beach this morning, and he was really quite upset. He wouldn't let that show in public of course but it broke his heart to see such a wonderful creature washed up on his patch because some ignorant ass hole hadn't disposed of their crab line properly.

Maurice, gabbling away with righteous fervour really wasn't improving Tony's day.

Tony loved his town, and he was consistently understanding and tolerant of all the people who came here. He did his utmost to act with grace, charm and diplomacy. Truth be told, he was a far better ambassador for the town than virtually all the self-appointed, pretend do-gooders.

Maurice wasn't aware of the depth of Tony's perceptions. Tony listened to the words and nodded accordingly as all his intuition told him, "We've got a wrong 'un here" Tony switched off his hearing for a second and allowed his other senses to tune in.
He didn't vocalise it, but he knew somewhere along the line, Maurice was protesting a little too much. Vocally, Maurice was righteous and indignant, but Tony knew, Maurice was hiding something, and attempting to hugely overcompensate.

Tony listened patiently absorbing every nuance

and tell-tale piece of giveaway body language as Maurice continued to rant. He knew if he just paid attention long enough, the weaselly pillock would betray whatever his secret really was.

Maurice was coming to the end of his diatribe. Tony decided to re-join the conversation. "…......and I think they should all pay a visitors surcharge when they come through the tunnel" Maurice was saying. Tony nodded in agreement.

"Right then Maurice, you let me know what happens eh? I have to go and sort out the roof on the workshop"

Maurice seemed satisfied. "Oh, okay mate, see you tomorrow? I'll be down my usual time"

As he walked off, Tony reminded himself to find some urgent work as far away from the seafront as possible tomorrow lunchtime. Maurice's crusade to deal with the 'toilet issues' was a rather tired and repetitive saga and despite his charm and diplomacy, Tony really didn't give a toss any more.

As he walked back towards the workshop, Tony spotted the banana yellow Jag which belonged to Denzel Sprygelly. It turned the corner on the approach to the seafront. Tony ducked inside the workshop doorway and decided he needed to be elsewhere.

Few people got under his skin like Denzel and his super inflated sense of his own importance. True enough, Denzel had fingers in many pies, but just as Tony had recognised in Maurice, he knew Denzel was a wrong 'un.

He allowed himself a smile at Denzels personal numberplate. DS-CB

The CB stood for Companion of the Bath apparently. Denzel had received the award in the Queens last birthday honours list. Tony wasn't sure what that meant, at best he could hazard a guess, some sort of royal soaper-upper perhaps? Perhaps the CB got to work alongside the Groom of the stool?

Knowing how Denzel operated, that seemed about right.

Denzel drove slowly across the seafront road noting just how many people had arrived since the schools had broken up. Denzel wasn't in the least bit worried about the mess these people made or the damage they did to the environment. Denzel was only interested in extracting as much money from these unsuspecting visitors as possible. if If that meant rigging games in his arcades and watering the overpriced beer he supplied to the camps, that was perfectly fine for Denzel.

In a minute he'd be driving past one of his fish and chip shops. That one was going particularly well this year. He'd done a deal to buy 'unfit for resale' potatoes from a supermarket chain just up the motorway.
"Every chip has six black bits!" was the local nursery rhyme. It didn't matter to Denzel, not a single resident used 'Denzel's Plaice'. It existed purely to serve the visitors and serve them it did. From 10am until 12pm seven days a week. Chips were £4 a portion, a pound more than his hourly pay rate to his staff, and 'Denzel's Plaice' sold hundreds of portions every single day. Life was good thought Denzel and then reminded himself he needed to make sure none of the staff thought they were entitled to a break on their 16 hour shifts.

Denzel still hadn't found a way to bribe Mark Wray, the local employment law compliance officer. At best all he could do was keep Marks inbox full of details of the unlawful practises of his rivals.

Mark kept trying to get more funds from the council in order to do his job properly, but too many councillors had a vested interest in not allowing that. It was a frustrated Mark who sat at his desk each morning reading emails appealing to the council for justice or the regular messages from Denzel snitching on yet another cafe owner.

Denzel absently pushed the buttons to open the soft top as his favourite Madness song began to play on the CD player "I like driving in my car" sang Suggs.
Denzel's revelry came to an abrupt stop as the interior of the banana yellow Jaguar revived the benefit of a full seagull air-strike.

Damien and Channella stumbled out of the pub and into the street. Channella belched loudly and simultaneously backfired. Several heads turned Channellas way and conversations paused as passers-by reacted with a mixture of horror and sniggering.

Channella decided to loose a second volley as Damien began to congratulate her on the first. River and Ocean peered at the doorway of the toyshop but there was no sign of the policewoman now. "Perhaps I can get back in for that Lego?" Ocean whispered to her little sister.

River thought this was a splendid idea. They'd definitely have to go back; she'd seen loads of things she wanted. Money wasn't to be an issue. Mummy quite often didn't pay for things in shops, so why should they?

The street was full of people. The noise was accompanied by the aromas of sand and sea-salt tang and stale urine. Ocean and River were looking forward to the beach. They'd had a great time last year and they knew there were at least five ice cream sellers within a few hundred yards. In addition to this, River had been planning her next adventure secretly for months. She was going to get one of those inflatable dingies and row herself and her older sister over the channel to the island. It didn't look very far. River was certain it would be easy.

Channella checked the time on her phone. That was about all it was good for here she noted. No signal. Didn't these people have Wi-Fi yet? She wanted to Instagram herself in her crop top and new pink leopard print leggings. There were two hours left before they could access their apartment, just time for a quick paddle, another ice cream and a short snooze on the sand. Channella was drowsy. Ten pints of Stella always made her like that. She'd better not drink any more until at least 4pm she thought. She discretely tried to let a bit more of her wind go, only to fail dismally and release a blast which could have rivalled the foghorn on the seafront.

The beach was surprisingly quiet. Thoroughly sandblasted families had sought refuge from the wind elsewhere. The wind was dropping now though, except for Channella for whom it was defiantly building.
Damien looked across the seafront taking in a bar, two licensed cafes and the two beach

shops the whole family had been banned from last summer. He doubted if anyone would remember them. He was wrong.

His gaze was attracted towards what appeared to be a four-foot-tall woman with a Green Army tattoo who was naked from the waist down. He gazed admiringly as the woman bent over to salvage a dog end someone had dropped. She picked up the lucky find and added it to her drolly tin. He'd half expected a flash of rusty washer so he laughed as he realised the woman was wearing flesh coloured leggings.

He wondered whether it would be okay to ask the woman where she'd bought them. His Mrs would look fabulous in a pair! Probably somewhere up market he guessed, like Aldi or Lidl.

"Just a paddle" Channella was telling the giwls "and don't go too far. Me and daddy will be right here" She plonked herself down on the sand with a thud.

Troy hadn't wanted to come back to the seafront just yet but their roll up tins were

almost empty and they'd seen plenty of dog
ends lying on the ground all over the seafront,
especially next to the public toilets.
One of Tony's colleagues was sweeping sand
and partially smoked cigarettes from inside the
seated shelters. Troy had asked if he could
take a few dog ends. The chap had gestured
towards a wheelbarrow and invited Troy to help
himself. The sand from the shelter smelt of wee
Troy noticed, but that wasn't going to put him
off. He greedily filled his tin.

In flat five Emmety Villa, Alan and Eileen were
discussing Maurice. "Yes", Eileen told her
husband, "Maurice was definitely upstairs again
when I came back this morning. His front door
was ajar, and I heard him come back down the
stairs and go back in" she recalled.

"Did you happen to see inside again?" Alan
asked remembering what he'd seen that time
Maurice had locked himself out and Alan had
helped him get back in.

"I didn't see any more rubber gear, but from the
looks of his kitchen table I'd say he's graduated
to frillies now" She threw her head back and

laughed.

Alan joined the laughter with her. Alan, a cousin
of Denzel's, worked for one of the parcel
delivery firms which covered the area. He knew
from the customs labels that Maurice had been
gradually building a personal collection of
bespoke studded rubber wear. There had even
been a few occasions while making small talk
with their peculiar neighbour, that they heard
what sounded like the squeak of rubber on
rubber. Presumably, Maurice was wearing
some of his wardrobe as they spoke.
Alan chortled "Christ! It's like living upstairs
from the cast of the Rocky Horror show" then
added "Frillies? What knickers?
Phaaahahahahaha"

"I know" Eileen answered between guffaws "I
wonder what he's planning?" Then in a more
serious tone "And what the hell was he doing
upstairs again? Poor Karen has had loads of
trouble with her guests bless her, do you think
he's doing something?"

"I really don't know" Alan answered "I know he's
amusing, but he's still a creep, I wish he'd go

back Bristol"

Alan and Eileen hadn't liked the look of Maurice from the day he'd moved in. Eileen had discreetly asked her cousin Lowenna if Maurice was known to the police. It transpired that he was very well known indeed to the station which covered his former address, although Lowenna hadn't been able to confirm why. Lowenna had asked if Alan was a 'special club' member? If he were, she'd explained, they'd be able to check out Maurice's background fairly easily. Alan was just about to be initiated into the mysteries of the club. He'd practised sacrificing chickens at his cousin Jago's farm, and he'd even bought himself a special tub of Vaseline, just in case.
The next meeting was next Wednesday, after that they both hoped to get a few more answers about their peculiar neighbour.

The town was as busy as a normal summers day. Ice creams were being dribbled, chips were being eaten, pasties were being plucked from the hands of visitors by seagulls, and beer was being poured and consumed in large volumes. The streets were crowded with people. Most of them seemed unable to differentiate between what was pavement and what was road. Frustrated but essential delivery drivers tried to go about their business while receiving barrages of abuse from people who wouldn't, in their home towns, have chosen to wander like headless chickens down the middle of a public highway.

Harassed shop assistants sold buckets and spades while trying to prevent similar incidents to the one involving River and Ocean earlier in the day.

The staff in the small supermarket did their best to remain calm and collected. The self-catering visitors from the holiday camps were probably the easiest to deal with. "No sorry we've run out of oven chips, yes and pot noodles" was enough to satisfy most of them. There were plenty of fish and chip shops, not to mention places for pasties. They hadn't really wanted to have to cook anything anyway.

Visitors like Monty and Camilla were a little more challenging. Their little cottage had a quaint kitchen, and although it was 28 degrees outside, Monty and Camilla had plans involving the open fireplace and the rug which laid invitingly in front of it. They might have thought differently had they known what Winston, a visiting Labrador, had left on the very same rug just two days before. Ignorance is indeed bliss.

Camilla and Monty had cornered a staff member by the wine fittings.
"Is this really the full range of Rioja? There don't appear to be any worthwhile vintages, if we give you a couple of pointers, can you order some in for tomorrow"
Mike took a deep breath as he composed himself.

"I'd love to offer you a greater range but we only have this small area and we're only able to order in what the warehouse has in stock." He explained. "There's a nice little shop where you might find a wider range in Truro" he added helpfully.
"Oh! So, you can't order us some, what was it called darling? Oh, I remember 'Vino para idiotas' then? "
Mike explained patiently again that he really didn't have any control over what the parent

company stocked. Monty interrupted him before he could finish "and where do you keep the Fois gras?" he demanded.

"I'm sorry, we don't keep Fois Gras, we have a good selection of other pates though, 12 types I think, would you like to see them? "

Camilla's bottom lip was trembling now "And I don't suppose you have any Dom Perignon either then?" she almost whispered. The horror! Monty had had enough and threw down his basket in a true luvvie style fit of pique.

"Well this just isn't bloody well good enough!" He shouted in Mikes face. Other shoppers stopped to watch in a puzzled voyeuristic trance. "Just how far is this Bloody Truro place? Can we walk there?"

Mike sighed, this was just the beginning, it was going to be another awfully long summer.

On their way to the seafront, Leafetta had thoughtfully picked up a case of blackcurrant cider. The back of the open delivery van had been too much to resist and her only regret was that she hadn't picked up two of them. 24 cans might last the afternoon, but they were bound to need more later. She wondered if the driver was still parked in the same place?

The sun was making her hot and she could feel her thighs begin to sweat inside her prized skin tone leggings. She'd brought four identical pairs on the 5 for 4 offers. £12 was a lot to part company within a single go, unless it was essentials of course.

Booze, fags, drugs and pies always had to take precedence over anything else. Since Troy had come along, he'd been giving her half the housing allowance he falsely claimed while still living at his mums. The extra £200 had meant Leafetta had almost completely renewed her wardrobe.
You could get a lot of great stuff at Primark for 200 quid.
Next month she was going to treat Troy to some new joggers, a brand new hoodie, and some of those leopard print man thongs she knew they always had.
They'd look like a couple of Toffs she reckoned. They might even let them back in Nandos again they'd be so smart.

Leafetta thought about her beloved. She smiled

as she remembered their first meeting. She'd
been out in the 'Muff' for a Friday night piss up
with her best friend Donna. They'd known one
another since primary school and recently had
a joint 22nd birthday party. Leafetta and Donna
were virtually inseparable.
Donna's real name was Michelle, but she liked
kebabs so much somehow the name had stuck.
By 2am they'd had about a litre of vodka each
and Donna was getting a little wobbly now.
They'd been asked to leave the third nightclub,
so they were catching their breaths on the Hoe.

Troy had been cruising in his metallic blue
Corsa. Troy knew he was cool, and he loved
the admiring looks all the pedestrians gave him
as he revved his engine at each pedestrian
crossing. A police car had pulled alongside him.
He'd try to shrink down in the driver's seat.
"Evening Troy, hope you're being sensible?"
the officers had said through their open
windows before continuing their circuit. Troy
had just stared ahead and then had to park up
by the registry office for another joint and a can
of cider.

From his parked position, he saw the taller of

the two girls crumple to the ground as Donna fainted.

There was an opportunity here. He quickly exited the Corsa and walked up to Leafetta as she leant over her inebriated friend. "Donna? Do you want this fag or not then? "Leafetta had been asking.

The collapsed girls handbag was lying next to her. "Hello sexy" he said looking Leafetta straight in the eye. She looked back into his bloodshot little eyes and felt a spark pass between them.

"Have you got a light mhet?" Leafetta had asked him.

"Na, sorry" Troy had lied "Try them by the bus stop, I'll watch your friend if you like?"

Leafetta had nodded and took a few steps towards the bus stop. I could be in here, she thought to herself. She wanted to say something witty to the Knight as she'd decided he was, after all, not many Plymouth lads had a Corsa any more, it was a classic!

"Do you fancy coming with us for a kebab later?" she said as she turned back to Troy. Troy was on his knees beside Donna and in his hand was the last £20 from her purse. For an instant, Leafetta was shocked.

"Oh what a bitch!" she said walking back towards Donna and Troy. "She said all she had left was a tenner and that I'd have to get my own drinks for once, what a cow! I'll tell you what, I'll go halves with you? "

Troy knew he was caught but this was too good an opportunity to pass up. "I'm going cruising up Elburton next, you wanna come?"

"You got anything to drink?" Leafetta had asked.

Troy had a bottle of white lightening on the backseat which he'd been saving for just such a day. "You bet he said"

Without looking back at Donna who was now burbling, Troy and Leafetta had walked hand in hand back to the Corsa. It was the beginning of what was going to be a fabulous romance.

Leafettas thoughts returned to the present. The bloke with the white tracksuit had been watching her. She pretended to spot something on the ground in front of her and bent over provocatively to pick it up. It was Damien's turn to experience hot sweaty thighs now.

Alan put the phone down with a flush of excitement. His initiation had been brought forward owing to the full moon they'd told him, and a desire to ensure that all members were flexible, and loyal.

He wondered which underpants he should wear. He hadn't mentioned the Vaseline to Eileen. It was a small sacrifice in order to open many doors he'd reasoned. Eileen didn't need to know the details and she already understood that what happened in the Old Gaol stayed in the Old Gaol.

Just a group of men pretending to be little boys was Eileen's perspective, with a bit of dressing up from time to time. Eileen calmly accepted that in this town, you simply didn't have to know everything which went on behind closed doors. Of course, you could gossip and speculate as much as you liked, in fact that particular activity was actively encouraged.

That time Uncle Piran had admitted he and Daphne were swingers had helped Eileen decide that some things were best left unspoken.

The rumour machine was generally rather good. If not, entirely reliable it was certainly entertaining, most of the residents would join in. But how did you get information on people like Maurice?

There was no alternative, Alan was going to join the club. It was going to be a night he'd never forget.

Monty and Camilla were now searching the town for its delicatessen and butchers. Sadly, they were at least 15 years too late. The townsfolk had long ago decided that they didn't want to support these small local businesses anymore. What was the point in shopping in your hometown when you could drive the 19 miles to Bodmin and go to a supermarket? It didn't matter that the quality was less and quite often the prices were higher. The 38 mile round trip meant you could buy a box of teabags for 20p less than in the local shops.

People were clever like that.

Monty accosted a young woman who was emerging from the bank lobby way.

"Are you a local? " He asked.
"Oi am my lovely" She replied with a distinct Brummie accent.
"Can you tell me where there's a decent off licence then?"

Sue, who had witnessed the incident in the supermarket earlier, recognised the man. She was keen to help.
"There's a brilliant little off licence just up Barbican Hill my lovely, just at the top. It's a bit steep if you're unfit" she picked her words carefully "But a young man like you ought to make it easily. I'll show you where to go if you like" she offered. She saw Monty take out his phone "It's called Tor View" she added helpfully.

Camilla, hopeful that they would find the all-important Rioja and Dom Perignon, decided to join the conversation. "And is there a nice delicatessen somewhere close too?"
"Ah well" Sue answered with a smile "you have to go right to the end of Hannafore for that one. It's called Portnadler"

Monty and Camilla were pleased. Tor View

didn't look that far away, and they could just stroll over the bridge to get to Portnadler. They thanked Sue and decided to tackle Barbican Hill first.

Sue exited the scene and went to join her friends in the Angling Club. They had a great laugh when she told them about the two rude visitors and their rudeness to Mike in the shop earlier. Everybody liked Mike. He was a thoroughly decent bloke.

Barbican Hill was known as Lung Buster Hill to the parents who had to trudge up twice a day to the primary school. Portnadler, as the name suggested, was a beach, not a delicatessen, and a good walk at that.
Sue and her friends laughed, and laughed and laughed.

An hour and a half later, Monty and Camilla were beginning to understand they must have walked past the off licence. The climb up Barbican Hill had been excruciating. Camilla was beginning to realise she needed to start doing Davina's workout again. Monty was doing his best to show how strong he was, which he wasn't, so he was failing miserably. Camilla would have thought him a weedy little squirt if it weren't for the fact that Monty's father owned his own catering business. Monty hadn't mentioned to Camilla it was actually a baked spud van. Camilla was bedazzled with the prospect of Monty's inheritance, and if that was what it took, she was prepared to suffer.

There didn't seem to be any shops where they were now. They'd passed a small parade of vacant shops, but these had obviously died. Now they were venturing down something called Sunrising, a direction suggested by another helpful local. Camilla was beginning to feel quite on edge. Now where the hell was the off licence?

Down on the beach Channella was snoring. Damien had left her where she was along with their hand luggage in order to get the giwls some more ice cream. They'd opted for strawberry this time.

The woman in the shop had been quite hostile, clearly, she'd remembered them from last year but perhaps not the actual incident. Damien flinched inwardly as he remembered the woman ordering him and his two 'mini Vicky Pollards' as she'd called them, out of her shop. Damien didn't know but for three decades the owner had run one of the most popular bars in the town. She'd never taken any nonsense, and she certainly wasn't about to now. He'd felt her eyes scalding his back as he'd walked away. Anyone else might have chosen to use a different ice cream shop. Damien hadn't made his name by making intelligent choices like that though had he? As he headed back to the sprawled figure of Channella, it occurred to him that perhaps he should have bought her one too? More money for beer later he consoled himself. Where the hell was that seagull going with Chanella's sandal?

Leafetta finished her sixth can and belched at the waves. The dishy guy in the white tracksuit was running across the sand. He appeared to be chasing a seagull which was trying to escape with something flattish hanging from its vicious beak. She turned her thoughts back to Troy and felt a flush. If they hurried up and finished their ciders, they could go back to their holiday apartment and enjoy some afternoon delight. She pushed the empty can into the sand and cracked open another one as she hummed the song to herself.

Troy had rolled them a nice fat one which he now lit. The home-grown weed released a cloud of rancid smoke which sent nearby families scurrying to get away from the stench. Troy knew no one would bother them here. He'd looked at some of the Looe Facebook pages and seen all the complaints about an absence of cameras or policing on the seafront.

He felt safe now. He knew that in a few minutes the icy hand of paranoia would grip him as it always did when he smoked the strong stuff. He pushed the thought away. What was important was getting wankered, no matter how bad it made him feel.
He looked at Leafetta as she opened him another can. As the mixed stimulants rushed through his bloodstream, he felt a familiar twinge. Soon it would be 'sexy time' again. He had a wonderful surprise for Leafetta. While he'd been urinating by the rocks he'd spotted one of those vibrating penis rings you could buy

from machines and in public toilets sometimes. It was a little sandy but a quick dip in a rock pool had dealt with that. It turned out that the little battery still had life in it. The only problem he foresaw was that it was a little on the large side and it might slip off. He decided he find some plasters somewhere and stick it on with one of those.

Just a short distance away, Damien had managed to retrieve the sandal and was making his way back to Channella when he spotted a different Seagull rummaging in one of the families bags. The gull withdrew its head clutching a packet of cigarettes. Damien made a lunge for it, but the bird was far to experienced to be caught. It took to the air and headed out over the water with its prize. Damien watched helplessly as another gull swooped down causing the thief to drop the packet into the water.

Damien wondered how many packets they had left now? Robbing his local newsagent had been a huge risk, but he and his mates had scored a couple of hundred packets not to mention rolling tobacco and then there were the two charity boxes, so it had been worth it.

He'd felt a little guilty as Peter, the owner, had wept when he'd seen the damage.
When Damien's dad had gone back to prison, Peter had given his mum a part time job and had been kind to his family at a time almost no one else in the village would speak to them. That had been bonkers too. Damien senior had been charged with running an illegal gambling ring. Damien junior had never understood why the racing guinea pigs had attracted the attention of the police in the first place. That was fen land life though. Things happened in the fens that didn't occur anywhere else.

Peter would get over it. He would get the door fixed on the insurance and replace the stock Damien thought.
Then he could go back and rob the place again.

He idly wondered what the prospects were here. He immediately dismissed the idea of checking out the ice cream shop he'd been in earlier. People like the woman who ran that place were far more serious than the police. There were some lines even Damien wasn't prepared to cross.

Damien made the bags as gull proof as he could and then went to the water's edge for a paddle with giwls. River and Ocean were waist deep in the water. "Look, that one's like a picnic bar daddy" Ocean pointed. Damien decided he'd join in with their enjoyment of 'spot and name', the floater game.

Channella dreamt blissfully of free beer and pork pies.

WPC Veryan was regretting her fourth cup of tea. So far today she'd been called to the scene of another underwear theft, the wrecked toy shop, and an incident involving a holiday maker who'd brought his pet Alpaca with him. The irate man had been unable to understand that he wasn't permitted to accommodate the beast in his holiday caravan.

There had been endless calls about the ever present aroma of weed in the town and Norman from Hannafore wanted to complain that someone had moved the parking cones from outside his house again.

Veryan had recalled the last incident. She'd explained clearly to Norman several times now that he wasn't actually allowed to appropriate a section of the public highway, even if his neighbours daughter did park there. The cones were an unlawful obstruction. Veryan wondered if the local council knew Norman was making use of their property. Norman was a tedious little man she thought, distant relative or not. Unfortunately, like a great many others, he liked to quote that he was a cousin of Denzel's, as if that gave him some sort of special rights. In some situations, in the town, this was actually the truth.

Veryan had to tread the line between family and duty very carefully. She wished her transfer to St Awful would hurry up and come through. Veryan was on her way to the Beach Shack now. The owners, who weren't related to Denzel, had a clean and private toilet they let her use when the need arose. Veryan knew all too well the horrors that lurked in the ladies toilets on the seafront, and she'd seen all the rats which emerged from the adjacent harbour walls in the evenings. Still, at least they cleaned up some of the rubbish the gulls missed.

Veryan had a soft spot for Tony too and so although she wasn't officially supposed to patrol the seafront, she took every opportunity to flirt with him. She'd been happily married to Mike for several years now, but in a world where she had to deal with the assorted incidents in the town every day, she just couldn't help herself. She needed her little fantasy.
She'd love to get him in the back of the patrol car and handcuff him. It wouldn't be the station she'd be driving to though; she had a quiet little spot down by Jewson's in mind. It was somewhere they wouldn't be disturbed she fantasised, and she could keep an eye on the doggers just across the car park while she was there. Perverts!

As she walked along the promenade, the strong smell of cannabis leaf greeted her. It could have been coming from any of a dozen places she noted as she glanced around. The beach was fairly crowded now but her trained eye immediately spotted the white tracksuit of Damien. Was he the one from that CCTV from last summer she wondered? He and his family had been reported over a dozen times, and with plenty of footage. The two little girls with him playing spot the turd certainly looked like the same pair. Veryan made a mental note to find out where they were staying.

She allowed her gaze to follow the line of the banjo pier and spotted another couple of candidates. It looked as if they were getting ready to leave. The short woman was pushing a cider can into the sand and the skinny one was brushing sand off his hoodie. Veryan wondered why the woman was naked from the waist down.

Maurice was back at home and selecting his evening wear. He heard the arrival of a vehicle; no doubt it was more 'Bleedy Emmets'. He glanced through the blinds. It was one of those things Scientists used to get around Antarctica.

There were four of them. Maurice groaned as he spotted the two girls. Maurice detested children. He didn't like people in general but he reserved special loathing for parents who brought their Mini-me's with them, objectionable little shits!
He'd have to collect some spiders from the

woodpile later and release them into the top apartment when the family went out for the evening. Maurice waited until the tribe had dragged the first of many cases up the long flight of steps and slipped out of door and around the side of the building.

Built into the steep slope of the garden was a cleverly constructed patio intended purely for visitors use. The owners of the building had discussed the construction of this at length with the residents. It was agreed that this side of the building and the presence of a hedge and wall would guarantee residents and visitors alike, both peace and privacy

A path of concrete slabs led from one of the side doors to the guest area. Maurice lifted three of the slabs and left them upright leaning against the fence on the edge of the lawn. On the underside of one of the slabs was a laminated notice Maurice had made the previous summer. "Essential maintenance! Patio out of use". Maurice made sure his notice was clearly visible from the side door the visitors would use.

Upstairs Channella had finished looking
through all the drawers and cupboards. It was a
beautiful apartment.
River and Ocean were using the beds in their
room for trampoline practise. They weren't
allowed to do that at home as Channella and
Damien had had to replace several beds
already. It didn't matter here though, let them
bounce she thought.

Damien meanwhile was standing on the kitchen
worktop with his head poking out of the skylight.
He guessed the view of the sea must be the
other side of the huge sycamore. He climbed
down again satisfied. Time for showers and a
change of clothes for them all before they
headed back into the town for dinner and in
search of entertainment.

The bar they'd been in earlier offered Karaoke
he'd noticed. He could do his usual 'I'm too
sexy'; Channella would probably have another
bash at 'Macarthur Park. The giwls would
undoubtedly do their version of 'Let it go' again.
Damien wondered if they'd have time to make
the ten pints again. He could always give the
giwls some money and then they could pick

them up from the arcade later.
Channella called through from the bathroom.
"Babes, can you help me? It won't flush. I think there's something wrong with the water"

No sooner had Maurice closed his door when he heard puffing and panting on the front steps again. He resumed his spot by the blinds and quickly recoiled as he witnessed the Plymouthian couple pause on the steps and begin eating one another. Troy and Leafetta were feeling amorous, and if they didn't get inside their apartment fairly quickly, then given the vantage point, half of Looe was going to be in for a shock. Maurice went back to his wardrobe and selected a purple gimp mask which he laid carefully in his special briefcase alongside his apron.

In their cottage close to the seafront, Monty was doing his best to remain calm while Camilla embraced full drama mode. They'd walked miles and still not found the off licence. They both had blisters, but Camilla's were life threatening. She was especially distressed at the poor quality of the Welcome bottle of Chablis she'd found in the fridge. She'd looked it up on her phone. Châteaux Marcon, 1985,

available in Waitrose for £55 a bottle.
Despite her disdain, all except a dribble at the
bottom of the bottle was inside Camilla now.
Monty was making himself busy unpacking and
ironing their crumpled clothes as Camilla
continued whinging. "……. knew we should
have gone to Padstow……." She half sobbed
and half screamed.

Monty had ordered a special delivery of
champagne and oysters from a local restaurant
earlier in the week. They were due to be
delivered at 4.30. Monty prayed silently they
would arrive early. When Camilla had a drama,
each minute felt like an hour. Monty knew that
his best tactic now was to keep filling her up
with alcohol until she fainted.
In the morning, hung over and amnesic, he'd be
able to convince her they'd had a wonderful
time.

Channella had managed to shower and change
herself and the two girls before the water
pressure mysteriously dropped again. The nice
chap who'd come to check it out said he
thought there must be a problem with the
pressure in the mains. He said it kept going off

at this time of day on a Saturday. Perhaps someone further up the pipe was topping up their swimming pool every Saturday? It was a mystery.

Damien had had a quick once over with a wet wipe and changed into another tracksuit.

Downstairs Leafetta and Troy were sleeping after their vigorous workout. For almost three minutes, sounds of intense intimacy poured out through their open windows clearly audible to anyone within earshot. Fortunately for everyone, it was all over quite quickly.

Maurice was having a snooze too. He had a busy night ahead.

In the shop where Mike had so patiently dealt with Monty and Camilla earlier, tempers were frayed. A seemingly endless stream of sunburnt visitors and their obnoxious children fought one another to get through the doors. The poor staff members who had to work on that shift had already faced several hours of rudeness and abuse.

Some of the locals had noticed that the

manager and his deputy were rarely present during these busy times. It didn't say much about supporting the staff or demonstrating leadership. No wonder most of the locals chose to go elsewhere.

Mike was serving on the till whilst mentally composing his resignation letter. He'd have laughed if he'd known the two colleagues, he shared the shift with were doing the same.

Mike had planned his escape for almost a year now and had worked diligently towards it. He'd wanted to open a record shop, but he knew that was unrealistic in a small town. Instead he had rented a small unit up by the seafront and had decided to provide the town with a much needed delicatessen.
He smiled inwardly as he recalled what Sue had told him a couple of hours earlier about that snooty couple and Portnadler.
He knew when the sign was unveiled next week it would send a shock wave around the town. It read.

"Never mind the Emmets! A local shop for local people!"

Mike had had enough of rudeness and abuse. He wondered what Denzel would think. He'd managed to secure the lease with no input from Denzel whatsoever so given his history, Denzel would undoubtedly show up and attempt to throw his weight around. After years of abuse in the little supermarket, Mike wasn't intimidated in the least by the thought.

As he waited for his most recent customer to finish packing pizzas and blue fizzy pop, he glanced up at the screens which showed the CCTV feed. In the corner by the wine fitting, two, he estimated, 12 year old girls had just taken a bottle of prosecco and were busily putting it into mums beach bag as the oblivious woman searched for something in the cheese fridge. Mike knew he'd view at least another half dozen similar incidents before the evening was over. It all seemed rather pointless. The company had told staff not to intervene if they were in any danger. The police didn't pursue prosecutions anyway. He didn't blame Veryan of course, how could he? He knew she did her absolute best and was as frustrated as he was. In the five years they'd been married they'd shared quite a few Emmet induced tears. They'd talked about leaving Cornwall, but then realised the far side of the Tamar bridge was where most of these unbearable people had come from. They'd eventually settled on working for the next ten years with gritted teeth and then retiring to Bodmin Moor. They'd reasoned there were places on the moor where even the locals didn't talk to one another, that was where Blisland had gotten its name.

Mike continued to serve customers with practised automaton like composure ignoring the tutting and grumbling. There was a crash from the back of the shop and Mike looked away from the till in time to see his poor colleague Jimmy having what looked like an Vienetta being crammed into his face by a customer. The customer must have taken it out of the packaging in the shop which was weird. Mike hit the panic alarm button.

In the main street the supermarket alarm joined the other voices in the
5 to 6pm chorus. It was always like this at this time of day. On the quay the Fire service and Coastguard were trying to get past middle of

the road walking families to attend emergency calls. An ambulance squealed its way up the hill out of the town. In the various car parks half a dozen car alarms all peeped away and were ignored. Car horns sounded, exhausts thundered and an assortment of children had melt downs and tantrums all the way from the bridge to the seafront.

What had once been a peaceful community centred fishing town was now competing with Benidorm and Ibiza to become a real life version of Purgatory.
Teenagers teenaged, Chavs Chaved, Cockneys Cocknied and Denzel Sprygelly worked his way around his establishments repeating the mantra he insisted all his staff learn "Just keep smiling and taking the money"

Mike had abandoned the till in order to help the bewildered Jimmy. A youth in a baggy pink vest with the legend 'Newquay. Lifeguard' was about to sock Jimmy again, this time with a trifle. Mike recognised the youth from the night before. Jimmy had refused to serve him and his crew with cider as they were clearly no older then 14. As the youth lunged Mike deftly stepped into his path, plucked the trifle from his hand and with a gentle tap to assist his momentum, propelled the youth head first into the open freezer door.

There was a gratifying thunk as the lads forehead collided with the edge of the door. The youth bounced back surprisingly quickly and just in time to trip over Mikes outstretched foot. He went crashing into the cat food display. Mike reached down an grabbed the youth by his ear uttering a single command as he did so. "BE SILENT!" he growled.

Veryan appeared magically beside him.

"Oh hello love" She smiled at Mike "As luck would have it, I was just outside, is that Kev P's boy?" She watched the boy flinch as he realised he'd been recognised. When his dad got back from sea later, he'd be in a world of trouble. He'd forgotten all about the CCTV when he'd decided to get even with Jimmy for humiliating him in front of his crew last night. The seafront skaters they called themselves. The seafront scroats was the name they'd been given by the other residents. Veryan knew them all, and all their parents. The boy began to cry.

Alan was pacing. He was due to meet his initiator at 7.45 at the doors of the Old Gaol. With just under two hours to go, he was beginning to get nervous. Eileen had already left their comfortable flat to go and watch a band with her sister in Polperro. Alan and Eileen usually went out on a Saturday. It meant not having to listen to the sound of the visitors and their late-night barbecues. It also meant that generally, Alan and Eileen were in a cider enhanced sleep when the visitors began arguing and door slamming.

On the occasions when they were woken up, Eileen would make them both a cup of tea while Alan played 'J'taime' and 'Just the two of us' quite loudly for an hour. That generally did the trick. If the rowing and door slamming was still going on, they'd call 101.

Alan hoped things would be quiet tonight. Eileen was going to stay at her sisters and as he still didn't know what his evening was going to bring, he felt that he might need a little alone time later.

He checked again to make sure the Vaseline was still in his pocket. The more he paced the more he had to keep hitching up his Mabyon Kernow Y fronts. He hoped he'd chosen something appropriate. Eileen had bought them one Christmas as a joke. Neither of them had thought he'd actually wear them one day. They were too good to throw away though. Everyone knew that the volunteers in the charity shops used to love to rummage through the donations and then have a good laugh with their friends. For a small town, apparently it was staggering how much rubber wear turned up. If only Maurice had known Alan thought, he could have saved himself a fortune.

In the flat below, Maurice was preparing for his evening too. He lay in the bath enjoying the satisfying scent of Ylang-ylang coming from his face pack. He'd have to move in a minute and finish shaving his legs and arms. Maurice remembered the scene earlier when the girl from the top apartment had come to his door to ask if there was something wrong with the water. He smiled as he dipped a large plastic jug into the bathwater and began to rinse.

Troy and Leafetta had woken up too. It was hunger that had brought them back into the world, they hadn't eaten for almost 3 hours. Troy was looking through their luggage for his best trainers. Troy was determined to look swish this evening. They were going to visit the Social Club they'd noticed on the Quay. They had a good chance of being able to scam some beers in there. Leafetta had bought a ring for £3 in the cancer shop as the staff had been too vigilant for her to be able to purloin it. They were going to pretend they'd just gotten engaged. Troy wondered if it was a good time to mention he was already married. He'd been separated for 5 weeks though so it probably didn't matter now. Then there was his first wife, she'd moved to Torquay. Technically they were still married too but he didn't suppose it mattered either. He wondered for a brief second how his children were. He was 24 now and at least two of his girlfriends had fallen pregnant every year since he was 15. This was one of the reasons he kept moving to a new house so often. Not that a squat or a mate's mums sofa was real moving house, but it made him harder to find.

Passing their lounge window was a couple roughly the same age as him and Leafetta. Troy recognised the little girls from the beach earlier and the cool bloke in the white tracksuit was the one who'd been chasing the seagulls. Troy waved. Channella caught the movement and turned to smile at Troy and return the wave. She abruptly remembered her missing tooth and so trying to hide it, rolled her tongue stud seductively across her lower lip.

Alan watching this from his kitchen window, was reminded of a wildebeest with a piece of bubble gum. Troy was bedazzled. He heard Leafetta break wind loudly from the bedroom and decided it was time for some more loving before they hit the town.

In their cottage on the seafront, Camilla was at last asleep. Monty knew this as he could hear snoring coming from the bathroom. He'd gone to the chemist to get some painkillers and some soothing foot gel. The oysters and champagne had arrived while he was out. Camilla had obviously been hungry bless her.

She'd eaten all but 2 of the two dozen oysters

and almost a whole bottle of Tabasco sauce. She'd polished off the champagne too, so Monty had run her a bath and left her propped up with a towel to stop her slipping.

On his way back from the chemist, he'd almost gone back into that appallingly inadequately stocked shop they'd been in earlier. There was a police van outside, and a youth was being loaded into the back when Monty passed so he decided against that idea. Instead, he'd knocked on the door of one of the closed restaurants and asked if he could buy a couple of bottles of Rioja from them.

The young woman who'd opened the door had explained that they weren't open for half an hour and they definitely weren't allowed to make off sales.

Monty had explained it was an emergency and offered to pay double the already hugely inflated price plus £20 for her trouble.

Monty got his wine. Sophie rang the correct amount for the two bottles through the till and pocketed the rest. As the owner always said, business is business!

Monty knew it would be at least an hour until he could wake Camilla and see her safely to bed. He wondered if he ought to pop out quickly now and get her another bottle of champagne? Once she was away, he could visit a few of the pubs and go for a boogie in the town's solitary discotheque. Monty knew his way around the town's bars and restaurants well as he'd been visiting for around 20 years. He was accustomed to hotels though, and ones with room service at that. Going shopping and having to fetch things for himself hadn't been a major feature of Monty s life. He'd always made a point of dating wealthy young women fresh from their private schools. He was 40 now and the application of regular moisturiser was paying off. He'd moved beyond the private schools and targeted wealthy university graduates now.

In his working life, Monty skippered yachts on private charters around the Mediterranean during the summer season. The rest of the time he was a suave and convincing freeloader. He generally had half a dozen excuses at his disposal which led to his prey handing over the reins to their cash flow. Monty liked not having to pay for things himself, so if that sometimes meant dramas like Camilla's, he was prepared to accept the rough with the smooth.

He put on some music to get him in the mood for his evening, Quincy Jones , Soul Bossa Nova, his favourite. Then he opened the second bottle of Rioja, it could breathe while he fetched the champagne. He'd better get another £500 from Camilla's cashpoint account too; he was down to £400 now and that certainly wasn't going to last. He'd checked her balance yesterday and Daddy had put her £25'000 a month allowance in so that would be fine. She didn't know but Monty also had a card for her savings account. He'd set up some direct debits on that one to cover his car payments. The rent for his flat in Bath was covered for the next four years so he didn't have to worry about that. That had been taken from the account of his last girlfriend. It was only around £100'000 so he knew she'd never notice.
Monty set out for the champagne. Life was going quite smoothly now.

Lowenna parked the police van by the RNLI

station on the seafront. The boy in the back had stopped sobbing now and had adopted a defiant attitude. Lowenna knew that after a few hours he'd have piped down. No one enjoyed being driven around for hours while she picked up a few drunks. Saturday evenings were generally spent in the larger towns but tonight her patch was to receive special attention. Lowenna had been able to liaise 10 extra bodies and four extra vehicles for this evening. It was time to show a presence and rein in some of the locals. The boy in the back was just one example.

Lowenna had extracted his name, he was more commonly known as Whistle, which was understandable as the poor kids' parents had decided to christen him Wilhelm. Whistle and his crew of 13 and 14 year olds had gradually occupied the seafront as the last crowd of dopers and skaters had approached an age where they could legitimately use the pubs.

Lowenna resented the graffiti and broken bottles they always left. She also had grave concerns about the safety of some of these kids. There were several predators who took far too much interest in some of the young people. Lowennas uncle Graham had been one of them, her uncle Norman another, and her Uncle Keith was yet another. Uncle Keith was still at liberty to enjoy the seafront, but Lowenna knew full well from Ob's that Uncle Keith like to cruise the gents. He did so with great regularity. In between he would sit drinking cans of strong lager in the shelters the skaters and their chums used.

Cousin Denzel might well be a money grabbing exploiter but at least he didn't try to befriend the children he paid £3 an hour. He certainly didn't sell them stinky weed or charge them for going into the shops and buying their booze. Lowenna checked her thought process. The only reason cousin Denzel didn't was probably he hadn't thought of it as a way to make money yet.

Lowenna didn't have to wait long. One of her plain clothes colleagues appeared with a handcuffed Uncle Keith and loaded him in the back of the van. Lowenna stayed in the front of the van out of sight. Apparently the inebriated Uncle Keith had been skipping along the cliff path with his pockets pulled out and his penis flapping.

"Look at me" he'd been calling "I'm a beautiful seagull, look at my lovely beak"

Uncle Keith had been picked up numerous times for exposing himself. It had been difficult to get a conviction so far as most of the people he'd exposed himself to had laughed or just plain refused to make a statement. When he wasn't busy flashing and getting sozzled, Uncle Keith was often found frequenting the auctions and antiques circuit, so Uncle Keith knew people who knew people.

Uncle Keith was in for an uncomfortable evening and Lowenna knew he'd have to be escorted to his favourite toilet several times. She could have just dropped him off at the local station and locked him in a cell, but she wanted him to get the full benefit of several hours in the back of the windowless van. Out of courtesy to her poor colleagues in the back, she decided she would keep swapping them every 20 minutes.

Just around the corner, Denzel was busy

counting £20 notes in the back of the bookies he owned. In the background Herb Alpert & The Tijuana Brass played a taste of honey.

He'd had all his managers as he laughingly called them, bring the days taking up to 5pm for his inspection. 'If you want to make them feel important, give them a title' was what Billy Butlin had said. Denzel knew the truth of it. He reckoned he'd have just enough time to bundle the substantial pile of notes before he had to get changed for the evening. Tonight, he knew, a new member was to be initiated. That meant something incredibly special for Denzel, it meant someone new to manipulate. He'd already played a major role in the enticement process. He wondered whether he ought to wear his red outfit, or the special purple one. Purple was the colour of Judges, and Denzel really really wanted everyone to know just how important he was.

Denzel had worked hard to get where he was today. In his younger days he'd had to kiss a lot of bottoms and knife a lot of good people in the back. These days it was his bottom that was being kissed. Like many of his ilk, he still enjoyed a good knifing occasionally.

Leafetta and Troy had met Channella and Damien properly in the queue for the fish and chip shop. It didn't take long to establish they were staying in the same building and that they had quite similar interests. Leafetta was busy befriending the giwls hoping this would inspire Troy. She had no idea he already had at least a dozen children.

Troy liked Leafetta a lot, but in the small gristle like globule which inhabited the space where most people had a heart, he knew that soon they would have to go their separate ways. Meeting Channella and Damien was awakening something in him and his thoughts from earlier in the day were now barely a memory.

For the next week though they had a room and Leafetta had promised to buy him some new joggers, so he decided to stay the course at least for the next few days.

They sat on the wall opposite the chip shop shovelling chips and battered sausages down their throats. Channella and Leafetta had complimented one another on their leggings. Leafetta wasn't sure how she'd look in a pair of the leopard print ones but as they were still skin tone, she'd agreed to swap a pair in the morning.

Channella really wanted to go to the Karaoke and Leafetta really wanted to try and dupe some suckers in the social club. They agreed to meet on the visitor patio later for a few late-night cans and then said their goodbyes.

As they walked away from the chip shop, River was behaving strangely. It didn't take Channella and Damien long to work out she was trying to hide something from them. As it was evening, they'd let her bring the filthy old hot water bottle cover she needed to sleep. It had been a squirrel originally, now it looked like a window cleaners buffing cloth. Ocean was clearly in the know too and she tried to position herself between her parents and her little sister to prevent them seeing what she had.

Knowing there would be a major drama if she attempted anything in the middle of the busy high street, Channella wheeled the giwls sharply to the right.

"Come on giwls" she announced, "We're going to the toilet" and giving them no chance to protest, marched the two into the public lavatory.

The ammonia hit their nostrils first, something akin to having a bucket of chlorine thrown in one's face.

Far too many unspeakable things had occurred in that small enclosure to describe here, and they'd only been thoroughly cleaned 20 minutes earlier.

Channella had to wait as three of the four cubicles weren't fit to enter, not even by her customarily low standards. At last her turn came and she ushered Ocean and River into the small space and closed the door.

Looking River firmly in the eyes she demanded "Show me!"

River dipped into the squirrel and her little hand emerged with a very full Air Ambulance collection box.

Channella was relieved, she'd worried for a moment that River had caught a pigeon. She kept trying.

"Oh well done darling" she congratulated the now proud little girl. "Are you going to share it with mummy?" River wasn't happy about this, especially when Ocean joined in "Me too!" she shouted.

River's bottom lip began to quiver. Channella reassured her "It's okay babes, we're bound to find another one later. I'll tell you what, we'll share this one and you can keep the next one all to yourself" River liked that idea, so the lip trembling stopped.

"Pop it on the seat darling and see if I can get it open" Channella rummaged in her handbag for her flick knife.

Damien sat on a bench outside smoking a roll up and watching a couple from Brighton having a full-blown screaming row in front of a street full of people. Apparently the man had picked up the wrong Chinese take away order while she'd been busy looking at hats and now, on top of everything else he'd done wrong that day, he was going to have to find somewhere else to spend the night. Clearly the two had been drinking all afternoon and the row ebbed and flowed between insults, swearing and staggering. The couple seemed oblivious to the fact they were being watched by around a hundred people. Damien was thoroughly enjoying it. It was just like watching EastEnders.

Inside the Guildhall Market just to Damien's right another drama was unfolding. A rather large lady on a mobility scooter was demanding a refund.

"I bought ten o these when I wor on 'oliday here last year and this one dun't werk"

She tossed the 10p lighter across the counter.

Behind the counter the owner marvelled that someone could be so financially vigilant to wait for a whole year to make a complaint and bring said lighter all the way back from Bradford.

She politely placated the woman and gave her not only a replacement, but also a full ten pence refund for her trouble. It was only as the woman was leaving the shop that she spotted the pack of toilet rolls on the mobility scooter. She followed the woman out of the shop and was pleased to see Veryan on the other side of the road. She beckoned her over. The woman on the scooter was queuing for chips now. She explained to Veryan what had just happened.

"I'll deal with her" said Veryan "Can you isolate the CCTV for me please?" The shop owner said she could and left Veryan to it. From the messages she'd been getting from other shop keepers in the town, this was the woman who'd being going around town stealing all day.

Veryan radioed one of her colleagues and within just a few minutes the woman was trundling back into the market on her scooter protesting that she'd simply forgotten to pay.

It was remarkable the owner observed that she could remember a 10p lighter for over a year but a pack of 24 toilet rolls between her knees had completely slipped her mind.

Things like that seemed to happen quite a lot in this little town.

In the police control room, PC Larry Martin sent small excerpts off CCTV footage from that afternoon to Veryan's phone.
The woman on the mobility scooter was undoubtedly the one they had named 'The Obesecycle bandit.'

This week so far, she'd been busy in Padstow, Newquay and St Ive's before choosing to spend her weekend here. They had footage to prove it.
The control room had been tracking her on the town CCTV too and her busy day had unfolded before their incredulous eyes.

Earlier in the day, one of those blue pope-mobile type vans had parked at the back of the police station.
Gregory Marks was the name the vehicle was registered too. A tall skinny man and a large woman had climbed out and between them, unloaded a mobility scooter and some large bags from the back. The woman had then put another much larger dress on over the top of the one she was wearing. It became apparent later that this larger dress was in fact specially constructed with extra fat padding and four well

concealed pockets that were large enough to hold anything up to the size of a fox terrier.

The two had then locked the vehicle and with the woman mounted up, had literately rolled into town. The man had gone for a cup of tea in a cafe while the Obesecycle bandit set about her days acquisitioning.

She went to the chain store chemist first. In there she'd picked up two expensive gift packs of perfume, 6 tubes of preparation H, at least three packs of pink hair dye, and a pack of Tenna pants for men. She'd then exited the store without paying and met the skinny man by the war memorial. He'd taken her prizes from her and gone back to their car. She progressed down the street and added to her collection.

The CCTV showed the skinny man back in the police car park just as one of Veryan and Lowennas fellow officers had been about to drive out. The man had raised his hand and made a gesture that the officer later revealed, should only be known to members of the 'Special Club'. The same club Alan was shortly to become a member of. The officer knew by the gesture that the man was entitled to park there and so carried on about his duties, never once thinking that he'd be getting reports about the man's accomplice for the rest of the afternoon.

For much of the afternoon the lift and meeting routine had continued. In one shop the woman had stolen a litre and a half of gin. From the shop next door, she'd picked up two large teddy bears and a girls swimming costume. She'd gone around the co-op twice in the early afternoon and again at teatime. Each time she'd filled her hidden pockets. She did go to the till once to buy a lottery ticket. In the coffee shop, in front of about 30 totally oblivious customers, she'd stolen the managers lap top. By the time she'd gone into the Guildhall, the back of the pope-mobile was almost full to capacity.

Luckily for Lowenna, her plain clothed officers had picked up the skinny man at the war memorial. She drove slowly up the street to go and collect him. She'd have to inspect the seafront later she thought.

The woman, in the presence of Veryan and her colleague had tried to make a big fuss but promptly stopped when the owner of the market deprived her of an audience by closing the doors to the public. As they waited for a different vehicle to take her to a cell in Liskeard, Veryan tried to question the now mute woman. It was pointless, she was saying nothing. Veryan stepped away and was quietly discussing what approach to take now with her younger colleague.

Clearly she would have to be properly searched, but here and now wasn't the appropriate time or place.

The woman, still on the mobility scooter appeared to be scratching herself. Veryans male colleague blushed and looked away. On the Scooter, the woman produced a two litre bottle of ready mixed from an undiscovered pocket and began guzzling vodka and Fanta as fast as she could.

With the skinny man now loaded in the back of the van with Uncle Keith and Wilhelm, Lowenna invited her colleague from the back of the van to hop out and get them both a cup of tea when they got to the kiosk at Hannafore. The three numpties in the back were securely handcuffed and seat belted.

Kieran, the young PC hopped out at the kiosk and Lowenna told him "Back in a short while, just going to do a couple of circuits"

She turned on the radio, Alan Moorhouse, That's Nice was playing.

She drove up Marine Drive about 20 yards and turned right into Portuan Road. She drove along Portuan Road for about 20 yards and turned right back onto Marine Drive, then she drove back up the same part of Marine Drive before turning right again, and she went around, and around and around.

Uncle Keith would probably be feeling quite car sick by now she thought, so she did another half dozen circuits before she stopped to let Kieran back in to the van.

"Right then" she said brightly "Tea!"

Lowenna instructed Kieran to drop her back at the war memorial where she was due to meet Veryan. Most of the evenings activities had been planned and now was the time to rein in a few more of the little scroats.

She reluctantly told Kieran to drop the three

clowns in the van off to cells in Liskeard and then to come back. It was going to be a busy night.

As Kieran drove off, she was surprised to see PC Veryan riding though the car park on a mobility scooter. It wouldn't go in the car Veryan had explained, and it was quite good fun. They had a few minutes before the next phase was due so Lowenna decided to give the machine a try out for herself and giggled all the way around the car park.

Channella paid for a round with small change, it was at least two hours until the Karaoke began so they had plenty of time to get ready. Ocean and River had gone to one of the arcades, they had plenty of money. The air ambulance box had contained almost £80. She expected the two giwls to come back empty handed but at least it wasn't their money they were wasting and it meant she and Damien didn't have to entertain them.

In the social club Leafetta and Troy hadn't made any friends so far. They paid a pound each for temporary membership and then received a hostile reception when they tried to sit at the bar. Clearly those stools were reserved for certain club members only.

Leafetta had decided to give it her best shot though so she clambered onto one of the empty stools and attempted to begin a conversation with the barman and the only two other drinkers in the place.
The taller of the customers had pink eyes and was swaying slightly, he'd probably been there all afternoon. She tried him first.
"It's nice here isn't it? Me and my bloke just got engaged and we're thinking of having our wedding here" She thrust her pudgy hand towards the man to show him the ring. On the other side of the room, Troy, having finished studying the juke box, moved towards the fruit machine. £100 Jackpot! The sign said. He fumbled in his pockets for change.
The tall man ignored Leafetta and called to Troy
"Sorry mate, that machine is for full time members only."
The barman joined in "That's right mate, like Dave says, it's for permanent members not

temporary membership, sorry."

Troy stopped fumbling and turned to the bar. "How much is membership then? Do we get a concession? We're students" he remembered to add.

Dave turned towards Troy "Oh yeah. What are you studying then?"

Troy didn't miss a beat "Horticulture and hydroponics" and then added "And my Mrs is going to be a teacher, so how much is the membership?"

Dave, the barman and the other customer burst out laughing.

The barman looked at Troy again and answered "That's fifty quid each for the year then, have you got your UCAS cards on you?" The three men began laughing again.

Leafetta was good at sniffing out opportunities, she also knew when to cut and run. She clambered down from the stool and crossed the room to join a now irritated Troy. As she took another swig of her watery club strength Carling said to him "This is pointless, This is more of an anti-social club than a friendly place" then added "It's these Cornish, they're nothing like us" They decided to drink up and try their luck in the pub they passed on their way along the Quay. It looked like it had potential. Strange name, The Harbour Moan. It was actually the Harbour Moon but earlier in the day, a seagull had dropped a frond of seaweed on the rooftop lights which spelt out the name and that was the reason the o looked like an a.

Before leaving the social club Troy urinated all over the floor in the gents and then un-spooled a toilet roll, shoved the mass into a pot and pulled the flush.

He came out from the toilet in time to see the one called Dave teetering down the steps. Just before he reached the bottom he stumbled. It was the fastest Troy had ever seen Leafetta move, but quick as a flash, she stepped in and stopped Dave from falling into a jumbled heap. For a moment Dave and Leafetta looked like a tangle of arms and legs but they managed to separate.

"Mmm, sorry" Dave offered and headed out of the door.

"You go steady love" she called after him, and then winked at Troy as she raised her right hand to show him the wallet she'd just so niftily extracted.

"Oh well done love" Troy congratulated her "Perhaps it was worth it after all?"

Clasping one another's pudgy hands, the set off for the harbour Moan.

In Happy Dolphin Cottage, Camilla fumbled in her hand bag for her pills. Monty had been quite lovely and had made her comfortable in bed and brought her a super skinny mocha with almond milk and sprinkles. Maintaining her act, Camilla had burbled that she wanted him to go out and have a good time. "I'll be fine" she said and "I'm sorry Monty, please just go and enjoy yourself"

She found the strip of pills and popped two from the foil. These were special, they weren't on the market yet. It was only because daddy owned his own pharmaceutical company that she had them. In 20 minutes, Camilla knew there wouldn't be a trace of alcohol left in her system. A mere two bottles were nothing of course. At her girls' school in Marlborough, all the girls had been expected to be able to cope with at least four bottles of Champagne in an evening. Camilla had won the house cup for her year and had impressed everyone, including the Dean, by managing 7 and still being able to park her MG. She hadn't had access to the pills back then either. It was probably the greatest of her accomplishments.

The pills had an added bonus that they also completely eradicated any chance of a hangover. She never went anywhere without them. One of the reasons daddy gave her such a generous allowance was that she was quietly marketing and distributing the pills throughout her social circle. The pills weren't cheap, and it meant daddy could skip and then falsify the trials data.

Camilla took out her phone and swished the screen to the tracking app. She'd put the tracker in Monty's wallet weeks ago and he still had no idea. It was especially important she knew where he was. Camilla had plans for the evening too. Monty was nice but what Camilla really enjoyed was a bit of rough. She didn't mind if they were 70 and could barely walk as long as they smelt of roll ups and did as they were told. She knew it wouldn't take her long, and she could be back in bed and fast asleep well before Monty staggered in.

Lowenna and Veryan were busy. They had changed out of their uniforms, but they were still working hard. So far, they'd taken six cars off the road and six drivers were now in the back of the van. For weeks the boy and girl racers had been burning through the town at speeds hugely in excess of the 30 and sometimes 20MPH limits.

These clots really liked to draw attention to themselves with their loud exhausts, thumping, so called music and reckless endangerment of both pedestrians and other road users. Lowenna knew that they were also frequently the killers of cats and other poor animals which had the misfortune to stray into their paths.

The ages of the detainees had surprised her. Three were in their early 20's but the woman with the black customised Smart Car was in her fifties. The two other blokes, clearly mid-life crisis types, were in their 40's.

With her colleagues placed in strategic locations around the town, the moronic motorists had been logged, filmed and then apprehended when they'd gone for the customary cruise around one of the car parks. They were going to be busy for a little while yet, and Lowenna had a few registration numbers on her list that she was particularly looking forward to seeing.

Lowenna checked her watch. Almost 7pm. She'd arranged to meet the town Mayor and several of the local councillors on the seafront. Hundreds of complaints were being made about the youths who gathered there and the way they intimidated passers-by, not to mention all the bottle smashing. There had even been an arson attack on the workshop.

The Mayor and several of the other dominant figures didn't seem to want to take any responsibility, so Lowenna had decided to force the issue.
She would only be able to have their company for about 20 minutes, apparently there was an important function they were all attending this evening. 20 minutes ought to be enough.

The rendezvous was at Denzel's Plaice and

Lowenna was pleased to see five assorted councillors and committee members waiting for her. She wondered if any of their family members would be engaging in the usual seafront shenanigans. That would be embarrassing, but it would also help to get them focussed.

From the shelter by the granite obelisk, clouds of pungent smoke drifted across to the group. Lowenna suggested that they go there first. As they approached the front of the shelter a group of about 20 youths hurriedly pulled up hoodies and collars and headed away as fast as they could. About half a dozen lads and a couple of girls remained, obviously not realising who this group of adults was.

Lowenna spotted Tony, her sisters youngest passing an enormous spliff to no less than Lydia, the mayors' daughter. As she strode confidently towards the group, she heard shouting coming from beach. A young couple were frantically calling for help. Lowenna spotted the object of their concern immediately.

Two little girls were rowing out to sea in a 4-foot

inflatable boat for all they were worth.
Lowenna felt her stomach somersault. All
thoughts of the smokers left her mind and she
burst into a run towards the RNLI building.
Luckily the lights were on and outside some of
the crew were washing down a rib from an
earlier shout.
Inside a large crowd had gathered to watch
Polperro Fisherman's choir sing with The
Fisherman's friends from Port Isaac

Lowenna's arrival caused quite a stir, she
quickly explained what was happening. Four of
the crew lifted the rib complete with outboard
and ran with it towards a slipway which led onto
the beach. Lowenna followed.

River and Ocean were having a wonderful time.
The man inside the shop hadn't noticed Ocean
untying the little inflatable boat from the big
display. His full attention had been on River
who had made herself busy emptying crystals
from a cabinet marked 'Please do not open'.
They'd found the oars by the Kayak rack. The
rowing was far easier than they'd expected, and
it seemed as if their boat was just steering
itself. They bought a six pack of fruit shoots and

picked up two packets of Jaffa cakes each. It was going to be fun on the island they'd decided. In their excitement, they hadn't noticed that the waves were getting bigger.

As Lowenna watched from the shore, it seemed to take the lifeboat crew a lifetime to reach the little girls. They were past the end of the Banjo now and moving dangerously close to the sharp points of the White Rock. At last the rib reached them and the crew lifted the girls to the safety of the larger vessel.

As the rib headed back along the river toward the boathouse, Lowenna looked back towards the place she'd originally been focussed on. As she walked back up the beach, she passed the young couple who had raised the alarm. She paused to thank them, but they had their own hands full now. Their little boy didn't want to go home just yet, and little Noah usually got whatever little Noah wanted. He'd learned exceedingly early that the way to accomplish this was a good tantrum. He was currently in full flow and winning.
Lowenna continued on her way.

Up by the shelter things had clearly gotten out of hand. The mayor's daughter was trying to pull the mayor off one of the youths who he had pinned to the ground. Another youth was inside the shelter cowering and nursing a bloody lip. The other councillors were having individual rows with each other and with some of their younger family members.

Lowenna was dismayed, this hadn't been her plan. She took her radio from her pocket and then called for assistance. On arriving at the shelter she did the only thing she could, she arrested the mayor.

While Lowenna was busy loading the mayor and the remaining youths into cars and vans for transportation to temporary accommodation, the lifeboat crew had docked.

River and Ocean had barely touched the concrete before they shot off along the quay and disappeared into the back streets. The lifeboat men were flabbergasted. Usually they rescued people and they were either appreciative, in shock or remorseful. The two little girls hadn't been any of these. On the trip back down the river they'd evaded any questions about their parents, and now, before a proper investigation could begin in to why they were at sea on their own, they'd fled.

Two of the crew had attempted pursuit. The girls, well-practised in running away, had no problem escaping. They didn't go back to the pub where Damien and Channella were. Instead they had dived into the door of a different bar.

The place was packed. Few of the adults noticed the girls were there. It wasn't long before both girls had picked up unattended glasses of cider and were huddled in a corner behind a pile of speakers.
They were sad about the jaffa cakes, but as they hadn't paid for those either, they reckoned it would be pretty easy to get some more. The pool table looked interesting and no one was playing at the moment. Ocean liked the fizzy apple taste and she wanted to do something fun. River tugged at her sleeve and pointed at something which looked like it was a control panel for a spaceship. There was also a box of electrical leads in the corner with them. After a quick discussion, the girls decided to plug a few

things in and see what happened.

Maurice was making the final adjustments to his clothing. On his stereo, Henry Mancini's Baby Elephant walk played. It reminded Maurice of the good old days before he'd been forced into retirement. He used to play it at his parties. Maurice also used to play it whenever he trying on a new garment in his 'room of mirrors' .
Henry finished and Bert Kampfert began his turn,

"A-weema-weh, a-weema-weh, a-weema-weh, a-weema-weh
A-weema-weh, a-weema-weh, a-weema-weh, a-weema-weh
A-weema-weh, a-weema-weh, a-weema-weh, a-weema-weh
A-weema-weh, a-weema-weh, a-weema-weh, a-weema-weh"

He smiled as he straightened his tie. He looked almost as smart in his morning dress as he had done in his uniform. He reached into the wardrobe and took out a purple rubber studded dog collar which he added to his case. Thank goodness he'd remembered.

Under his suit, his rubber one piece felt snug and reassuringly moist against his smooth skin. He'd opted for the shortie this time. He loved the full body outfit, but he'd almost fainted in the car park when he'd worn it for the June meeting. Much as he enjoyed being sweaty, something cooler was required at this time of year.

Maurice would walk through the street and no one would know the ecstatic feeling he enjoyed knowing what he had on underneath, and just how good it felt.

He just had one quick job before he left, he needed to pop up to the shed and gather a dozen or so fat spiders to release into the two holiday apartments before he went out.

Maurice had already seen Eileen leave and he knew full well where Alan was going to be at 7.45, oh boy was Alan going to get a surprise. Maurice knew his role was important tonight, everyone's was, but he was confident that he could arrive in plenty of time and still get all his little jobs done. There was a small thud which passed through the building. Maurice knew that was Alan's door. He was on his way.

Monty showed his membership card to Debbie who had taken over the bar in the Social Club. "It's okay love" she said "I remember you, are you still drinking Guinness? "
Monty smiled appreciatively. He usually stayed in one of the hotels close by and he liked to give people £20 tips which generally meant they remembered him. Of course if he'd been giving away his own money, he might have said a 'keep the change' if it was only five pence, but certainly not anything higher.

A tall bewildered looking man teetered into the doors.
"Did I leave my wallet here?" he interrupted.
"Haven't seen it Dave" Debbie replied "When did you last have it?"
"Hrrumph, well I bought a pint just before I left, I've only been as far as the Grumpy. By the way, the downstairs bog is flooding out onto the street"
Dave muttered something to himself about having dropped it on the street and he'd better go and look.

"Oh bye then Dave, good luck" Debbie called after him.

She turned her attention back to Monty "Guinness then?"
"Yes please" Monty answered. She was a pretty little thing he thought and then immediately began to wonder whether she had any savings. He'd have to buy her a few drinks and bung her a couple of good tips to draw it out of her.

As she reached behind her for a glass, Debbie clarified her assessment of the waxy guy at the bar. Clearly, he had charm, obviously a yachty from his clothes, probably drove some sort of sports car. He'd probably try and chat her up. She'd just let him waffle like all of them and nod and smile in the right places. She had to work anyway so she might as well extract a few drinks from him. She laughed inwardly. Twerps like this one always really fancied themselves, and they were so easy to play because of it. She turned and gave Monty her best smile, "Would you like one yourself?" He asked. She smiled again, she loved this game, and like most of the bar staff in the town, she knew how to play it so much better than Monty.

Alan waited anxiously on the doorstep of the Old Gaol. He was relieved to see Denzel approaching. Almost all of the other 'Brothers' had already assembled and were waiting inside. Denzel had explained that usually everyone entered by the back door but on occasions like this, only the candidates and their introducers would use that entrance.

Alan and Denzel entered and Alan was led to a special preparation room. Maurice slipped in through the front door and went straight to the main changing room. It didn't take Maurice long to get ready.

Denzel had already explained to Alan that he must follow all the instruction to the letter. They'd had a brief rehearsal the previous weekend. Alan signed a document forfeiting his house and all his property if he backed out now. Denzel told him he could have the paper back after the ceremony and that it was just a formality.

Inside the preparation room was a small table, two chairs and a mirror. On the wall some coat hooks had been mounted. There were two boxes on the table. Aside from that, the room was empty.

Denzel indicated one of the boxes.

"You need to take off all your clothes and put that on. The other box is mine"

Alan peered into the box. It contained what looked like an old hessian sack with a hole cut in it, presumably for his head.

"Everything?" Alan asked, the tremor in his voice clearly audible

"Keep your scuddies on" Denzel answered, "Let's face away from one another as we get changed shall we?" It was a command rather than a question. Alan hadn't looked to see what was in the other box. He wondered what Denzel would be wearing. He was greatly comforted that he'd been allowed to keep his underpants. Some of the videos he'd watched on you-tube had indicated that might not be the case. Thank god they'd just been nonsense he thought. He began to do as he'd been instructed.

"Don't turn around until I leave" Denzel instructed "Then wait here, and someone will come.

Alan focussed on getting changed. As he slipped the rough sacking cloth over his head, he heard the door to the room click shut as Denzel left.

On the other side of the town, Troy and Leafetta were making new friends. Their engagement story was working. Most of the other customers were from a wedding party themselves. They were the colleagues of a local girl who'd been married that day. About 20 of her workmates and their partners had been told to join the party at 7pm. They'd politely queued outside the venue and then at 7 precisely had trooped in and delivered all their cards and wedding presents to the happy couple.

At ten past seven, there was a flurry from the two families who rapidly cleared away all the remaining food, and all the booze including everything the new arrivals had brought with them.

Apparently the party was over and so instead they'd congregated in the 'Moan' as Troy still thought it was called, and tried to work out what the hell had just happened.

Leafetta worked the room shoving her charity shop ring under peoples noses.
Troy and Leafetta hadn't realised, but people were buying them drinks just to get them to go away.

Up at the bar a beleaguered looking Dave was asking if anyone had handed in a wallet.
Leaffeta caught his attention as he was about to leave.
"You okay love?" She asked "Would you like one of these? "She indicated several full half pint glasses of Carling.
Lifting his wallet had been simple, she was going to finish the job and get his roll ups now.

Alan almost leapt out of his skin when the door clicked open again.

"Look at your feet and only your feet and put your hands behind your back" a firm voice instructed.

He felt his wrists being tied together

"Now bow your head" A cloth bag of some sort was pulled over and Alan lost sight of anything except his toes. He felt a heavy loop of rope as a noose was pushed over the head bag and down to his shoulders. Alan relaxed a little, Denzel had told him this would happen.

He was about to be murdered.

"Put a gun against his head, pulled my trigger now he's dead"

Damien was giving it his best shot. While the rest of the customers winced, Channella looked on proudly. Damien was doing superbly considering how little he'd drunk, just seven pints and he was belting it out with all the finesse of an amorous walrus.

The ghost of Freddie Mercury looked on from the side of the room and put his hand over his face to try to shut out the horror. Since he'd passed, thousands had massacred his masterpiece, but this was a tragedy equal to

the very worst of 80's pop music.
Surely the guys doing the Karaoke would pull the plug in a minute? Freddie wondered if he'd be able to short out the electrics.

Camilla ordered a white Russian at the bar and eyed up the white track-suited Damien as he gave his all. Someone like him she thought, or maybe a bit older. It was much easier to get away from the older ones. Camilla had noticed Channella and in particular her flesh coloured leopard print leggings, £3.50 from Primark. Camilla had invested in a tiger stripe pair which she'd picked out especially for this evening £84.99 from a little boutique she liked in Bath. Both pairs had been made in the same sweatshop in Karachi by seven year olds.

Camilla saw how Damien gazed at Channella, as did most of the other men in the room. She was confident her outfit was drawing similar looks. Behind her came the sound of a loud face slap. Apparently, someone's wife had noticed an ogling man too.

Camilla checked her phone. According to the tracker, Monty was in the Social club on the other side of the river. He was probably trying to make friends and play pool she thought. She hoped he didn't let his imagination run away with him again. In Dartmouth, a few days earlier he'd been telling a tale all about how he helped Chay Bligh sail around Southern Argentina. It turned out that one of the parties just happened to be Chay Bligh's son.

Monty had been promptly ejected from the wine bar and had narrowly avoided bashing his nose several times on another chap's fist. Monty had that effect on people.

In the Old Gaol, Alan was led along a corridor and into a dimly lit room.

He sensed the presence of other people, but he couldn't see anyone. He was ordered to kneel at the base of some carpeted steps.

"Alan Higginbottom, you have been brought here of your own free will. Is this correct"
Alan remembered his coaching

"I have Grand Master"

"And do you willingly accept the role of Hiring-my-biff?"

"I do Grand Master"

"Then you must accept his fate" The voice boomed. There was something so familiar about the voice but Alan just couldn't work out who it belonged to.
The Grand Master continued.

"Hiring-my-biff, you have been found guilty of the crime of divulgence, do you accept your fate?"

Once again Alan answered the rehearsed line. "I do Grand Master"

"Let him be slain" The Grand Master ordered.

Alan felt something brush his head three times as somewhere in the room, someone knocked loudly three times on a piece of wood. Denzel had been very clear about this next part, so trusting he was doing the right thing, Alan allowed himself to topple backwards, as if he were indeed dead.
To his considerable relief, two pairs of hands caught him and he was lowered onto a canvas sheet. The sheet was gathered up and wrapped around him.

Alan knew he had to remain motionless until he was 'reborn'

The assembly of brothers began a strange chant.

Tinky winky woo
Winky pinky doo
Trinky lanky bonk
Spinky tanky zonk
Rinky dinky doo
Winky wonky moo.

This continued for several minutes. Eventually after the strange verse had been recited around 20 times, a gong sounded. The chanting abruptly stopped.

The familiar voice continued.

"Arise Brother" Two pairs of strong hands helped Alan back to his feet.

"You have been reborn. Do you solemnly swear to keep the oaths and secrets of the brotherhood until you shall depart this world, and accept death by having your throat cut if you betray this oath?"

Alan felt something press against his throat. "I solemnly swear" Alan answered. What he really wanted to do was satisfy an overwhelming urge to go to the lavatory but that would have to wait. He clenched. Whatever had been pressed against his throat was taken away.

"Brother Alan, you are now reborn into our fellowship, come back into the light. You may remove the head covering."

Alan felt something cut the bonds at his wrists and shaking loose the cut rope, reached up and took off his mask.

He was in an enormous cave like hall lit only with candles. In front of him, the Grand Master extended a hand. "Welcome" In his other hand he held out Alan's brand-new apron.

Alan's head swam. He'd know that gimp mask and dog collar anywhere. The Grand Master was no less than his peculiar neighbour.

Looking resplendent in gimp mask, dog collar and a bright purple rubber Shorty body glove, it was Maurice.

Alan limply extended his own to take the proffered hand. There was cheering. Now his eyes were adjusting, Alan was able to see to his astonishment, that Denzel was standing beside him holding a stone masons' mallet. That wasn't what shocked Alan though; he'd expected something exactly like it.

Denzel was dressed in a Santa outfit. The man to his left, presumably the owner of the second set of hands which had caught and then lifted him, was wearing a wonder woman outfit. He also clasped a sword. Alan felt his knees weaken; the sword looked alarmingly real.

Before he knew it, all sorts of people were stepping up to slap him on the back and shake his hand. Quite a few of them seemed to favour a mixture of fancy dress and assorted rubber wear. Some just had fancy dress. The really disturbing ones had gone full bondage gear, plus aprons of course.

Alan shook hands and tried to remember all the names. He was staggered at just how many of these people he already knew. Martin from the post office had come as Snow White, Bill from the garage was Sonic the hedgehog. Paul from the spar shop was Alice in wonderland. Alan

didn't recognise the Incredible Hulk or Osama
Bin Laden. The roll of fame went on and on.

Debbie was relieved more people were coming
into the bar. Monty had been waffling about his
recording studio in California. Debbie thought
that the truth more likely was that the closest
Monty had probably ever been to California was
watching Bay watch.
He'd paid for two drinks for them each and she
was bored now. She wanted him to leave
before any of the more proprietorial locals
decided to take matters in to their own hands.
The last time she'd handed him his change he'd
clasped her hand and looked her in the eyes
while he told her what beautiful hands she had.
She'd laughed, and then immediately washed
her hands.

As he was clearly a fantasist, she'd decided to
play along with him. She told him all about her
wealthy Uncle Denzel who owned half of the
town. Uncle Denzel was dying she said, and
she was only here tonight because she needed
to get away from the hospice for a few hours.
She was going straight back after work. Uncle

Denzel had named her as his successor and so she was going to inherit everything.

Debbie knew all this was nonsense of course, but she had sometimes wondered if her uncle would leave her anything. Debbie didn't know but Uncle Denzel had told all his nieces and nephews they were his favourite. It made them easier to manipulate. Monty was clearly spouting rubbish and Debbie didn't want to reveal any genuine personal information so she was happy to spout rubbish back.

Monty was still waffling "....he sent me a text just the other day actually" he was saying. He'd been talking about his friendship with David Bowie Debbie was trying to remember if Facebook had told her that David had died, she was fairly sure he had. She allowed Monty to continue embarrassing himself.

Further along the quay, Leafetta and Troy were leaving the 'Moan'. Leafetta was flushed with success. Not only did she have Dave's wallet and roll ups, she also had his chewing gum, his keys, a small torch, a packet of tissues, a piece of string, a biro, his phone a comb and a small model of a post van.

She finished going through the pockets of the jacket. She'd taken it when Dave had gone to the toilet. Troy had followed Dave into the toilet when he'd failed to return after a few minutes. Dave had clearly fallen asleep in a cubicle and was currently snoring. She tossed it over the quayside into the water along with all the stuff they'd decided was useless.

Dave was going to be in a lot of trouble when he eventually got home to his wife.

Troy had noticed that one of the boats was tied right next to a ladder which was set into the granite blocks of the quay. Troy was feeling amorous again, He nudged Leafetta "How about on a boat then?" he pointed.

"No way" She laughed "I'll ruin my leggings on that ladder"

Troy could see she had a valid point "Let's find that other couple then?" He suggested "Where did they say they were going"

Leafetta, relieved she wouldn't have to climb
the dangerous looking ladder answered
"I dunno what it's called, but they said they had
karaoke"
As they looked across the river, Leafettas eyes
found the fish market building.
"That looks quiet" she smiled and gave troy a
lustful look "How about in there?"
Leafetta enjoyed her alfresco lovemaking and it
would make a wonderful romantic memory, her
and Troy on the fish quay at Looe.

In the police station, Lowenna hung up the
phone and turned to Veryan "Oh well, we might
as well go home then"

"What did he say?" Veryan had been hovering
while Lowenna rang the assistant Chief
Constable.

"He said the mayor was a good friend of his
and that he couldn't believe he'd attacked
anyone, let alone a minor"
Lowenna was exasperated, she knew exactly
how this would play out. "He's sending down
someone from Plymouth to take over the shift
and we're to go home."

Both Lowenna and Veryan knew that by the time they came back on duty, the mayor would have been released and all the paperwork would have vanished, including the call logs to control and their notebooks. It was always the same when they arrested a 'special club' member.

"Mike doesn't finish until late" Veryan offered, "fancy a drink?"

"That sounds like a splendid idea" Lowenna answered "Anywhere but the Galleon, it's Karaoke tonight and it'll be full of drunken idiots"

"It's Saturday night" Veryan answered with an eye roll "Everywhere will be"

They laughed.
"It's a nice night" Veryan continued "We could get a bottle and sit on the blocks by the beach"

"Really?" Lowenna answered with a broad smile, and jokingly "have you got some weed then?"

They laughed some more.

Outside the Old Gaol a figure dressed in dark clothing climbed back down the fire escape. She'd listened at all the doors and windows, but the place appeared to have been thoroughly soundproofed. All the noise from police cars, particularly on the seafront earlier, had served to mask any noise she'd made. Not a single chink of light had escaped the heavily covered windows. She knew her quarry was inside; she'd followed him from his house and then watched him go in. While she waited, she'd taken lots of photos of the other 'Brothers' arriving. She knew she'd have to wait a while, and then she could follow her subject again. If she was able to, she fully expected to learn that Maurice was up to his old tricks again.

River and Ocean had plugged in all sorts of cables. Some went to the mixing desk, some to the lights and the rest went to the speakers. The girls had worked out there was a junction box which led to a main power cable. That had something which looked like the transformer on their computer at home on it, so this must be the main switch. Now was the moment to flick the switch. Ocean finished her cider and reached forward.

The effect was spectacular, the red and blue lights flashed and the boom which came from the speakers could have felled a giant. As the stunned customers staggered and flinched, tables were upset, glasses dropped and beer sloshed liberally in all directions.

The bar staff along with several of the customers had ducked right down thinking an aeroplane must have crashed into the building.

The backing track for Smoke on water blared out.

At the end of the bar Rock-star-never-was and legend in his own imagination 'Tom the axe Bleaufeld' looked in horror as sparks began to pour from the tops of his side fill monitors. "The fire in their eyes kaaaapooooff!" went the one on the left. Frightened customers ducked and screamed as pieces of speaker flew across the room.

Ocean and River decided it was great fun, but it was time to leave. The two little girls quietly slipped out from the pandemonium.

Troy and Leafetta pulled their clothing back up and as she leant forward to pick up her bag, Leafetta noticed a red light winking from the rafters of the fish market. She looked around, there were three more, all working apparently. She huffed. You couldn't go anywhere these days, flippin CCTV cameras were everywhere. She took the opportunity to throw a few old tissues and chewing gum wrappers from her bag onto the floor.

It was almost dark now. Troy felt a lot more comfortable in the dark. The fish market had been deserted when they'd arrived although they could hear a mixture of music and beery voices from the bar just opposite. They'd entered through the heavy plastic fly curtains on the water side. Troy was about to start looking for anything worth stealing when Leafetta pointed out the cameras. He wondered whether their passion had been recorded. He dismissed the idea. It was unlikely anyone would look at it unless they had a specific reason to. They decided that just this once, they'd leave everything else alone.

In the Galleon Channella was basking in the applause. She'd crucified Macarthur Park but nevertheless, most of the men in the room were cheering and wolf whistling. Most of the women in the room were shaking their heads in dismay. One or two were wondering where Channella had bought her leggings and if they would have the same effect on their men if they wore them at home.

Camilla absently wondered if she should have a go but she was being chatted up by a sleazy looking old codger. She was doing her best not to keep looking at his white slip on shoes.

He'd introduced himself as Cowboy which was fitting. Cowboy had half done building jobs all over the town. He clearly fancied himself as a lady's man. "I own all of Shutta lane" he'd told to her trying to sound important. Camilla knew how to play along and she'd given her glass a small wave as she smiled at him and said "Well you must be able to afford to buy me another drink then"

Cowboy had dutifully gone to the bar. He was like a little boy who'd been promised a puppy, putty in her hands. Camilla took the drink off him when he returned and leaned towards his ear whispering "If you get some condoms, we can go down to the beach"

Cowboy could hardly believe his ears. He nodded, put down his glass, checked his pockets for pound coins, and obediently set off towards the gents.

No one else was stepping up to the Karaoke hotspot, so Damien put down his free tenth pint, clambered to his feet and teetered over to the spotlight. He told the compare his chosen tune , took up the microphone, unzipped his tracksuit top to reveal his spindly chest and began warbling.

"I'm too sexy for my love
Too sexy for my love
Love's going to leave me

I'm too sexy for my shirt
Too sexy for my shirt
So sexy it hurts"

River and Ocean spotted daddy, River looked up at her older sister "Oh dear" She mouthed. Ocean answered. "Yes, it's embarrassing, let's find a drink and then go and find mummy." The two girls began searching for unattended cider glasses.

Lowenna and Veryan had been to say Hi to Mike. They'd picked up a couple of bottles of wine and some disposable cups. When they told him where they were going, he laughed. "Reliving the old days eh?" he quipped. For decades, the young people of Looe had congregated on the seafront on a Saturday night. In the 50's and 60's there had been a coffee bar which stayed open late. In the 70's the older kids had been able to buy beer in the off licence or cider at a local farm. Like so many other coastal towns, everyone's parents either worked or went out on a Saturday night. As long as no one seriously overdid it, it was just part of Looe life. The local bobbies would walk around occasionally and in general, everyone behaved. In the mid 60's, something else had arrived and there were far more locals than would ever admit, who had smoked their first joint on the seafront. Being part of the in crowd there was virtually a rite of passage.

Lately things had changed a lot. The youths who gathered there now had stronger things than cannabis on their minds. Empty bottles and beer cans used to get cleared up and put in the bins. At the moment the fashion was to hurl the glass at the concrete cliff reinforcement, the blocks as they were known.
Lowenna and Veryan were expecting things to be as quiet as a graveyard now though, especially after the events earlier in the evening. They could have a drink, wind back the clock, and reminisce about less complicated times. As they walked down the high street they saw Cowboy and a young woman in her 20's stumble out of the Galleon.

"Oh my god" gasped Veryan "What the hell is she wearing?"
Lowenna took in the tiger stripe flesh coloured leggings and silver high heels.

"Get used to it love" she answered "When you get your transfer you'll see a lot more" and then added "I thought the circus wasn't due until next month? That's Cowboy isn't it? I need to have a word with him, not tonight though, he's still at it I see"

"I just don't get it" Veryan replied, whatever do they see in him"

"I really don't know" Lowenna continued "And that time we had to strip search him last month his little carrot looked like it had been sat in the bottom of the fridge for months"
They laughed and from a discrete distance, followed Cowboy and Camilla toward the seafront.

Cowboy and Camilla had barely covered any distance when he abruptly turned into a side street "Let's go this way" Camilla none the wiser followed. That had been close. Cowboy had almost bumped into his Mrs. He hadn't seen her in the throng of people, but he'd heard her voice clearly. Her London tones had cut through the crowd to reach his ears just in time. Cowboy scuttled away quickly up the side street.

Knowing there would be fewer people walking this way, Veryan and Lowenna followed. Cowboy and Camilla arrived at the junction where the Old Gaol stood. They paid no attention, their thoughts were centred now on finding a little privacy between the rocks.

As Veryan and Lowenna approached the Old gaol, someone dressed in dark clothing slipped from the back alleyway across the street and huddled down in the gateway of the holiday apartments opposite. Both women spotted the black clad figure.

"What do you think?" Veryan asked quietly

"Probably another one of their flipping silly games" Lowenna answered. They dismissed the thought whoever it was might be up to no good and carried on their way.

Monty finished his gin and tonic and said goodbye to Debbie, maybe not this time he thought, but when he came next time he'd get to work properly. If Debbie was going to inherit so much, she'd need help with her investments.

He pushed a £20 over the bar towards her and slide off his stool "Thanks for really great service" he smiled "I'll see you again when I get back from Berlin"

Debbie thanked him and flashed a broad smile "Oh thanks lovely, yes, make sure you call in. I'd love to get to know you better" The thought made her flesh crawl, but she knew how to get his cash off him and the little twerp was going now so she'd won.
The smile might have looked genuine but Debbie wasn't smiling at Monty , she was smiling at herself.

From their vantage point on the top of the blocks, Veryan and Lowenna watched the pantomime going on below. The voices floated up on the night air. They could clearly hear Cowboy "I just need to go for a wee"

"Good idea" Camilla had answered "Me too"

Veryan and Lowenna could see them both in the moonlight but down on the shore line, the two would be lovers had lost sight of one another and every time one or the other moved, the rocks obscured them from each other. They tried calling but close to the water's edge, they couldn't hear one another above the lapping waves.

"Must have gone this way" Cowboys muttered as he set off eastwards towards Plaidy. Camilla was working her way around the rocks in small circles. "Are you there?" She was completely confused. He'd seemed keen enough. She huffed and decided to go back to Happy Dolphin cottage, there was still some champagne in the fridge, she could at least enjoy that before Monty came back, or perhaps she could go back to the Galleon and have a go at the Karaoke.

Without a proper farewell, Camilla and Cowboy went their separate ways. For a long while after Camilla had vanished, Lowenna and Veryan laughed raucously as Cowboy continued his pointless search in the dark. He certainly had commitment they noticed as his mutterings floated up to them.

"Are you over here? Oh, feck it, where did she go? I wasted two bleedy quid on condoms too"

Back on the high street, Michael Sprygely had just seen Troy and Leafetta go into the Galleon. He was still feeling bruised and battered and not quite himself, but he owed Troy a little something and so he followed them into the busy bar where he could keep an eye on them. Michael knew it would be foolish to approach them inside the pub, and so he got himself a pint and then watched them from a dark corner.

Blissfully unaware they had been spotted, Troy and Leafetta had walked in just as Damien was finishing

"On the catwalk, yeah
I shake my little tush on the catwalk "

They pushed through the crowd towards Channella who was listening with interest to the girls account of their evening.

Damien waited for his applause but the only clapping was in appreciation of the fact that he'd stopped. He made his way back to the table to find the new friends from the holiday apartments waiting for them.

"You were brilliant mate" Troy lifted his hand to high five Damien.

"Shall I get a round in?" Leafetta followed. They'd been delighted to discover that Dave's wallet was surprisingly full.

At the karaoke microphone, a Johnny Vegas lookalike began a version of Robbie Williams Angels. He was as tuneful as a Moose in rutting season. The audience seemed to like it.

Inside the Old Gaol, Brother Alan was beginning to enjoy himself. After all the back slapping, hand shaking and introductions, he'd been asked if he'd like to wear something a little more comfortable. He was led to one of the many smaller rooms which it turned out had two racks full of different outfits. There was a chef's outfit, a spaceman, a cowboy and all sorts of others. It was just like the changing room in Mr Benn. There was even a sign on the inside of the door which said, 'To adventures'.

Alan had chosen the purple wizards robe with the stars and moons sewn onto it. He particularly liked the pointy hat. A brother dressed as Frank N Furter led him back to the main hall where a feast was now being laid out by a small crew of smartly dressed waiters and waitresses.

Alan was invited to take a plate and be served second, after the Grand Master of course. Maurice led the way. There were sausages on sticks, jelly and ice cream, blancmange, all sorts of buns, a large trifle, iced gems and there was even a huge dish of cheese footballs.

There was also a vat of fruity punch which all the brothers wasted no time at all in guzzling. The punch it transpired was very strongly alcoholic.

Then they played games. Musical chairs was good and Alan was doing well. A brother whispered to remind Alan the Grand Master must always win.

That wasn't such a problem when it came to pass the parcel as it was Maurice who was controlling the music. Alan won. He unwrapped the last layer to find it contained an apron.

Someone had embroidered it with the words, I won pass the parcel in the Old Gaol. After that they'd played balloon stomp, beanbag toss, freeze dance and hide and seek.

Next came the dancing, the assembled punch fuelled brothers had a wonderful time doing the hokey cocky, and then everyone including the waiting staff had joined in with Agadoo. Later there was free style to a few Kylie Minogue and Status Quo numbers and finally Alan was given the great honour to lead a conga around the building.

All the while Alan kept slugging down the punch. He was going to feel lousy in the morning, but he was having so much fun, he just couldn't stop himself. The only brothers who weren't swigging down large volumes were the two who'd made the punch, Denzel and Maurice. Maurice had detached himself from the conga and had a quite word with Denzel whose turn it was to be on the music.

"I think it's time to show them god now then?" Maurice nodded towards the second vat which just being brought into the room by the waiters.

Denzel reached inside his mankini and pulled out the bag of magic mushroom powder he'd been holding for Maurice.

"I'll do it if you like?" he answered knowing full well that his job was to support the Grand Master in every way possible.

"Good lad young Denzel" Maurice reassured him "Keep going like this and you could go far" Denzel's piggy little eyes lit up greedily . He stepped across the room and tipped the whole bag into the large vat.

Maurice sat back on the Grand master's throne and indicated that Denzel should sit beside him. They didn't have to wait long until the first brothers began to experience the effect of the mushroom powder. Maurice had dismissed the waiting staff. As usual they all went away with their payment for the evening plus an extra £50 note each to ensure their discretion. There was a bus waiting in the car park to take them back to Southampton. Maurice liked the agency which was run by a brother from a different club. Keep it close and discuss nothing was a sworn mantra.

The figure lurking with his camera opposite had watched them leave and listened to their whispered conversations. In the past, she'd followed groups like this. She knew a great deal could be learned from their idle chatter. Back in Bristol, she'd even slipped in dressed as a waitress one evening in order to witness for himself the peculiar rituals.

The ruse hadn't lasted long, and she'd been ejected by the head chef. Thankfully, the lady had thought she was just trying to freeload for tips. The Brethren hadn't been informed of the uninvited guest. The head chef knew an abrupt end would come to that particular facet of her business if they had.

The music played on

"There's an old piano and the playing's hot behind the green door"

Brothers stumbled towards the benches which surrounded the room or sought out quiet corners, and gradually immersed themselves into their personal psychedelic worlds.

"You'll be owing me some money then" Maurice leaned towards Denzel

"Yes Sir, it's all in order, I left the case on top of your desk Sir" Denzel answered.

£40'000 in £20 notes had been counted and recounted and Denzel felt confident his scheming and planning had been worthwhile.

"Have you got the contracts?" Maurice asked, Denzel indicated a sack by his side

"Then let's begin shall we?" Maurice responded, and reached to his side to pull a small desk towards his throne. He took out his gold plated fountain pen from a pocket cleverly concealed in the lower portion of his rubber shortie.

"How about we start with solicitors and police officers?"

They laughed, the contracts the intoxicated brothers were going to sign had taken months to draw up. Once they were signed, Denzel and Maurice would be collecting a percentage of the rent for most of the business in town. Those

who weren't effected this way had other conditions written into all sorts of contracts and agreements.
Denzel and Maurice would very soon have a controlling interest of virtually every aspect of the small town.

Cowboy gave up the pursuit, he had no idea that Camilla had gone back to the Galleon. "Naw feck it!" he muttered repeatedly to himself.

On the top of the blocks Lowenna and Veryan watched as they swapped stories about various celebrities in the town. Lowenna was telling Veryan all about the time a News of the World reporter had photographed the wrong hotel and the story had gone nationwide with the headline 'Swingers Paradise'. The owner of the genuine source had been furious as the wrong hotel had appeared in the paper. By all accounts, the other hotels bookings had outstripped demand for the following two years.

"Look at the silly sod" Veryan pointed down to Cowboy. He was stumbling around trying to undo his flies again.

"Well, it's a lot more entertaining than a usual Saturday" Lowenna answered as she lifted the bottle to offer Veryan a top up.

"I wonder how Mikes getting on?" Veryan nodded and held her plastic cup out.
They both knew that Saturday nights could be rough on the staff in the small local shop. At least when things got really bad for them, they had colleagues with dogs and tasers. Mike only had his workmates and his courage. Veryan helped out whenever she could but in the summer, she always had to be in a dozen places at once.

In the Galleon, Camilla was in the spotlight
"Every now and then I fall apart
Turn around, bright eyes Every now and then I fall apart "

Troy rose to his feet and headed to the gents. On the other side of the busy bar room, Michael put down his glass and followed Troy out of the back door and along the passageway that led to the gents. He was just about to open the door when Michael caught up with him and laid a hand on his shoulder.

"I want to talk to you"

Troy turned and was horrified to find himself staring at the giant. He didn't have time to react. Michael put one large hand on each of Troy's shoulders and stepped towards the terrified little squirt.

Michael leaned close to Troy's ear and in a quiet voice said simply

"I owe you this".

He brought his knee up. Troy took a sharp inhalation and made a noise remarkably similar to the one Michael had made earlier. His hands shot to his crotch, but it was too late. Michael relaxed his grip on Troy's shoulders, the boy had gone from being pale to looking very green. Troy fell to his knees still clutching his privates, and was sick all down his top.

As a parting shot Michael said to him "If I see you again, you know what'll 'appen"

Troy nodded mutely and as the giant walked

away, crumpled to the floor and began sobbing.

Damien found Troy still curled up on the ground weeping. Between sobs, Troy had explained about his accident earlier in the day. He helped Troy to his feet and held him up while he completed the reason he'd left the bar in the first place. Damien was very understanding. Back at home he explained, things like this happened to him and his mates a lot. Their mission accomplished, they re-entered the busy bar.

Leafetta and Channella had a new friend. Camilla had joined the party. The girls were talking shoes and clothes when Troy and Damien reappeared. Damien gave a brief summary of what had occurred. Leafetta was sympathetic, but she'd learned there was a discotheque on the seafront, and she wasn't ready to go home yet.

Troy really didn't fancy going anywhere now, except to his bed. It was decided that Damien would take the giwls back to the apartment and chaperone Troy along the way in case he encountered any more misfortunes.

Camilla looked at the tracking app on her phone. Monty had been in the Social club, The Harbour Moon, one of the hotels on the west side quay and he was now in a pub on the east side of the river but still about half a mile away from Camilla. She thought it was probably unlikely he'd go to the discotheque so she might as well stay with the two new friends she'd just made. They clearly had a few different experiences, but deep down they all wanted the same things, a nice house, a half dozen good holidays each year, plenty of money and nice clothes. They all knew there wasn't any knight in shining armour, they were far too shrewd for that, more like a knit in shining armour they'd joked as Damien and Troy had left. They all knew you had to chase the money and find someone who understood your mostly dishonest way of life. As for romance and love, well, that was for affairs of course!

Camilla fancied that now the blokes had been dispatched, she and her new friends might well find a little bit of mischief.

Denzel was grinning from ear to ear. He'd gone

around the room and persuaded assorted brothers to sign their names on the bottoms of the new contracts he'd had specially prepared. He patted Alan on the head as he walked past him on his way around the room. Alan was sitting cross legged on a dais which led to an alter with his hands stretched above his head. He was gently swaying, and Denzel paused to listen to what Alan was saying.

"I'm a little elf" he said again and again. Denzel chuckled and carried on.

The brothers, despite their intoxicated state, were accustomed to following instructions when they were with the walls of the hall. Most compliantly signed the contracts and then slipped back into their fantasies.

Denzel finished and went back to Maurice. "All done, what about this lot now though?"
Maurice looked around the room. "Well most of them will just drift off to sleep and then go home in the early hours. I'll pop back in in the morning and lock up, no one would dream of coming in here"
Denzel knew the truth of that.

In his youth, he'd been brought up with stories of the sacrifices which took place in the building and several tales in which people had gone into the hall, and never come out again.
Most of the doors required thumb prints to activate them anyway so if anyone did get in, they wouldn't get very far.

Denzel thought about one of the contracts he'd just had signed. His warehouse was now going to supply all the soft drinks to most of the bars in the town. Denzel was happy.
"I think I'll stay for a little while" he told Maurice.

Maurice was more than happy, he had a case full of money to count and he had plans for later.

"Just make sure our new brother gets home safely" he gestured towards Alan.

Denzel promised he would escort Alan home himself. It was only fitting. The whole reason he'd invited Alan to join in the first place was that Denzel was absolutely smitten with Eileen. The more little jobs he could find for Alan to do, the closer he could get to Alan's wife, even if

she was his cousin.
For now though, he'd be a good friend and look after his chum.

In the main street, Ocean was adamant she wanted to lie down in the road and go to sleep. Damien was already carrying the unconscious River who was snoring loudly.

"Help us out mate?" Damien nodded at Ocean imploring Troy to pick her up.
Troy had no intention of picking up the little girl. He could see the lights of the taxi rank.

"I'll get us a taxi, hang on here" Before Damien could answer, Troy was on his way. He'd almost made it to the cab at the front of the line when a huge figure loomed out of the doorway by the adjacent kebab shop.

Troy recognised Michael. Michael recognised Troy. Michael casually placed his polystyrene box on top of a bin as Troy walked straight into his outstretched arms. Troy was too shocked to even pause. His thought process was so slow he simply continued in the direction he'd been travelling.

"Remember me?" Michael grasped Troy by the shoulders for the second time that evening, Troy experienced the repercussions of his carelessness.

Maurice stepped into the cool evening air and inhaled deeply. The evening had gone surprisingly well. Initiations were always good times to get things done. The £40'000 he'd just collected from Denzel felt satisfyingly heavy. The contents amounted to £2000 each for the 20 advantageous contracts that had just been signed.

Denzel would cover his costs and begin to see a clear profit in just a few months, and at that point, Maurice was owed some more money. As all the books went through the same accountant, it would be easy to monitor what was happening. Brother Roy, known to the other brothers as Robin Hood Roy, would make sure no one paid any more tax than they absolutely had to, and no one could evade their new contractual terms in dealing with Denzel either.

Of course, the entire business from their conspiracy in the first place was highly illegal. It had been Maurice's idea. Denzel might be ambitious but he lacked Maurice's creativity. If it went awry, they would certainly both go to prison for a very long time.
Maurice wasn't concerned though, the brethren included several police officers, the only ones he had to be careful to avoid were the Sargent, Lowenna, and her colleague, Veryan.

Women were a problem for Maurice. Unless there was some way to begin a special 'women's special club' it was a strictly all male affair. Given the antics of the brothers when they had their play times, that was probably just as well. Heaven forbid that wives and girlfriends should ever find out what the chaps got up to. Keep your friends close and your enemies closer was a phrase Maurice had learned the value of when he'd lived and slipped up in Bristol.

He turned his thoughts back to the contents of the case. A few more like that and he'd begin to replenish the pension he'd lost when he'd had to move to the town in the first place.

Taking his place as Grand Master of the local special club has been simple enough as most of his antics in Bristol had been kept well concealed from general knowledge.

Maurice already had a senior ranking in the hierarchy and was a twenty two and a half degree brother.
The timing was hugely fortunate too. No sooner had Maurice arrived than the former Grand Master had experienced a rather unfortunate accident and a vacancy had opened.

No one really knew the full story of what had happened with Grand Master Timmy except that he'd been found at his home as cold as an iceberg in a bath full of flakes, sprinkles and hundreds and thousands. One line of gossip suggested he'd topped himself.
Maurice was so wrapped up in his thoughts that he was oblivious to the darkly dressed woman who was now following him again.

Monty was still working on his circuit of the town. He planned to go to the Galleon next, and then perhaps the discotheque. Just because Camilla was unconscious didn't mean he couldn't enjoy himself.

As he got closer to the kebab shop, he spotted a youth with a Burberry cap rolling around on the ground moaning and clutching his privates. Standing over him was another youth in a white tracksuit and beside them curled up on the public benches, were two little girls.

The one in the white tracksuit saw him coming and asked "Can you help me get him into a taxi mate? He's had a bit of a rough evening"

Monty couldn't really say no and so between them they lifted the still groaning Troy and poured him, under the disapproving gaze of the driver, into the back seat of a seven seater cab.

As they lifted him in, they didn't notice his wallet slip from the pocket of his joggers and drop down into the road, neatly standing parallel with the curb. The wallet contained Troy's national insurance card, the ID card he had to show his probation officer and £200 which was a part share of the money Leafetta had stolen from Drunken Dave. It also contained Drunken

Dave's driving license, his Lloyds bank card and his Royal Mail ID.

Troy had thought these might be useful at some point and asked Leafetta not to ditch them. She couldn't see the point other than the contactless payment card. Troy knew that people rarely looked at photo's let alone names, and the ID card might well get him into places he couldn't normally go, like the big Plymouth sorting office. If he could blag his way in there, there was no telling how much gear he might be able to walk out with, even if it was just from the staff locker rooms.

Monty said goodnight and wished Damien and Troy luck as the taxi pulled away. It had only gone 200 yards when it did a sharp U turn in the road and came back to collect River and Ocean.

The heady aroma coming from the kebab shop was too much for Monty, he joined the queue.

In the Galleon, Channella, Leafetta and Camilla were screeching their chosen Bananrama song. Leafetta and Channella were too plastered to follow the words on screen and so while

Camilla held it all together, the other two just kept chanting the same phrase again and again.

"Robert De Niro's waiting
Talking Italian
Robert De Niro's waiting
Talking Italian "

The men in the room were transfixed. The din the girls were making had no effect on the men at all. Three pairs of skin coloured leggings though, it had been like holding up a plate full of sausage rolls in a room full of hungry Labradors. Most of the remaining women in the room were ordering their men to drink up. It was time to leave!

Leafetta and Channella were too drunk to sing, but along with Camilla, they could clearly see what effect they were having on the alcohol weakened mutts and they were delighted. At last, to the immense relief of the bar staff and the Karaoke crew, the appalling noise ended. The applause was deafening.

The landlord leaned over towards the MC and told him firmly "No more". The men were clearly loving the performance, but the noise was excruciating, and on top of that, the women were leaving as hurriedly now as if the place was on fire.

The MC announced the girls the winners for the evening and the landlord handed them a cheap bottle of Prosecco. In the past he'd given the winner, always a girl, a peck on the cheek. On this occasion he simply handed over the bottle, grunted "Well done" and quickly retreated.

Perhaps in the future he thought, he'd just have a real band. He used to be in a band himself. There were plenty around, the trouble was getting the band members to actually play something they all knew all the way through. There used to be a great local duo who would play, 'Intoxication' they were called. It all got a little predictable though and, in the end, the customers had known the running order better than the duo themselves. It was a tough one. The men had been hypnotised by the women in the flesh coloured leggings, but the punishment on everyone's ears was just too high a price to pay. At one point when Leafetta had caterwauled her way through 'You'll never walk alone', the MC had looked like he was going to cry.

Camilla and Channella went to the bar and asked for some clean glasses, meanwhile Leafetta opened the bottle and poured her third straight into her lager. "It all goes down the same way" she said with a wink to a customer who was looking on in alarm. The man quickly looked away and turned his attention to Camilla's tiger print which was currently being displayed to full effect as she leaned over a bar stool to reach for the glasses.
Around 40 other pairs of eyes were doing the same. The man Leafetta had just winked at tried to be cool and take a swig from his glass. His missed his mouth completely and poured half a pint of Rattler down the front of his best shirt.

Veryan and Lowenna dropped their empty bottles in the recycling box on the seafront.

"Poor Tony" Veryan was saying "If only the other people would use this"

Lowenna knew of Veryan's fondness for Tony, like many women in the town, she quite liked him herself. "How are you and Mike getting on these days?" Lowenna decided to direct Veryan's attention back to her husband"

"Oh we're fine now" she answered "I think he's gotten over his uniform thing now"

Lowenna understood. Her husband had liked it when she first had her uniform too. There were sometimes when he'd asked her to wear it especially. The whole performance was ludicrous. The last thing a WPC wanted to do to feel sexy was put on her uniform during her off hours. Lowenna had put a stop to that by insisting that she would put her work gear on if he put his on. Lowennas husband was a pest control officer for the council.

She'd passed the tip on to Veryan who then insisted that Mike don his supermarket outfit on a few occasions. The uniform requests had stopped and there was harmony in both marriages again now.
As they walked up through the street weaving their way between drunks, they laughed some more at just how ridiculous the whole uniform performance had been.

Damien carried the two little girls inside the apartment and quickly got them to bed. Troy had limped up the steps and ended the evening by inviting Damien and Channella down for a breakfast spliff.

"I'll leave the door unlocked" he said "Just come on in and give us a shout if we're not awake" In truth, Troy felt so bad he doubted if he'd be able to sleep. He stumbled inside the apartment and collapsed on the sofa. He fumbled with the remote control for the television, but it just wouldn't work.

Upstairs Damien was finding that he couldn't get the remote control for his television to work either. Maurice would have smiled. He collected dead batteries from anywhere he could. The cleaners for the holiday apartments had learned to check the ones in the remotes following lots of complaints. They also used to leave spares in the kitchen drawers. Maurice would wait until the right moment and then let himself in and swap the live batteries for dead ones. If the guests were particularly resourceful, he also had a supply of burnt out fuses so he could tamper with the plugs on the TVs or microwaves.

As if they'd been synchronised, both Damien and Troy drew out their phones and caught up with the world viewed through Facebook. Damien posted all the photos of the giwls he'd taken on the beach plus a half dozen deeply unflattering shots of Channella unconscious. He'd even remembered to take some video while she was drooling and snoring, he uploaded that to her page. She'd laugh about that in the morning.
The giwls were asleep now.

Troy looked at the intimate photo's he'd taken of Leafetta on the fish quay. He wondered if they'd ever have sexy time again, the way his genitals felt right now, it seemed unlikely. After a last quick look at his newsfeed, he drifted over onto candy crush and began mindlessly clicking.

In the Old Gaol, some of the brothers were feeling a bit more communicative and were comparing hallucinations with one another "It looked like the most enormous teddy bear" Robin Hood Roy was telling Alan, the wizard.

On a different bench, a few of the younger brothers, men in their 40's, were talking too. "I feel great" declared one still dressed as a giant squirrel. "I feel like I could dance like I did at all those raves in the 90's"
This was quickly followed up by another brother, this one attired as Elmer Fudd "Brilliant idea! Let's go to the disco"

Denzel was pleased. He'd been distributing CDs for his so-called friends to listen to in their cars. It had taken him weeks to learn how to combine playlists of tracks from the seventies and eighties with subliminal hypnotic suggestions.

He'd gotten the idea from a programme he'd watched about subliminal programming hidden in Disney films.
Walt had been a high ranking special club member too, and if it was good enough for Walt, it was good enough for Denzel.

In the end he'd had to enrol the assistance of a local radio producer.
It had cost Denzel a lot of money and he was also deeply indebted in terms of the favour bank all the brothers relied on. It had been

worth it though and although they didn't know it, most of the brothers were now responding to their programming. Denzel had trained them not to question anything out of the ordinary and just to go along with things he commanded.

Half an hour earlier most of the brothers had been so frazzled their consciousness had been enjoying their own personal Alice in wonderland experience. They were still intoxicated now, but they were behaving as if everything was perfectly normal. Not one brother paused to wonder why they felt so extraordinarily peculiar. Peter, who ran one of the garages in the town, was one example. "Yes sir!" He saluted Brian who was currently dressed in a tight pair of rubber shorts, studded neck collar and rubber balaclava .
"Purple dwarves with kilts on Sir, carrying blenders"
"Oh super" Brian answered "And will they be staying for tea?"

Other pantomimes were being played out around the room and Denzel loved it.
The group of would be disco goers was growing. One turned to Denzel and asked if

they were all done for the evening.

"All 8th degree brothers are free to leave now" he called out loudly and walked to the alter where he rang one of the dismissal gongs.

Obediently about half the brothers began to gather up their cases and undo their aprons. "If any of you lads are going dancing, you might as well keep your outfits on" Denzel told them as they prepared to leave.

As the room began to split, the lower degree members formed a pack of fancy-dress frippery equal to the best New Year's Eve party. The remainder of the group, the senior brethren, were the ones entitled to wear leather and rubber, and they did so, on every possible occasion.

Lowenna said goodnight to Veryan as Mike let her in to the now locked Co-op. "I'm almost ready love" he told her "I just have to put the papers out"

"Oh, I thought Jimmy did that now?" Veryan had been encouraging Mike to work only his hours and take his breaks. Mike though like so many people, constantly stayed on to do just that little bit extra. He knew in his heart that his bosses were laughing at him, but he just couldn't help himself. He answered his wife "Oh he would have but Tony and me were looking at the Corny Crimes" Mike named the local newspaper by its nickname.

Veryan knew what they'd been up to. "So who won?" she asked with a smile.

"Tony's still ahead of me, but we had three each tonight"

Mike and Tony had been playing this game for over a year now. Every weekend they'd get together and go through the local crimes and who's been in court pages. For every person they personally knew or who they'd spoken to, they scored a point. In a small town, they both knew most of the subjects of the articles, and so did Veryan, it was she and her colleagues who'd put them there.

She and her colleagues had a slightly different game, they would look at the marriage pages and see if there was anyone they'd slept with before they'd married themselves. Veryan and

Lowenna were on two all. One of their far more promiscuous colleagues had a far higher score. His antics were well known, behind his back he was referred to as either Chlamydia Clive or Constable Condom. Veryan could never understand his apparent popularity, as far as she was concerned the guy was a drip.

She took her husband's arm and they headed for home, it had been a very long day for both of them.

Lowenna spotted a group of teenagers loitering at the end of the small car park. Most of them weren't even 15 yet. She knew they all recognised her. They looked away as she got closer. "Have you lot been hanging around in the bank lobby again? I shall be speaking to your parents once I've checked the CCTV, which I'm going to do right now" she added in a slightly quieter voice.

She had no intention of looking at anything other than the backs of her eyelids now , but it didn't hurt to keep the young ones assured that she was watching them. The group suddenly realised it was time to get home, and quickly at that. They scurried away into the night.

Veryan looked up towards the taxi rank. There were no taxis. From where she stood, she could just see something odd leaning up against the curb where the front car always stopped. She went to investigate.

The queue for the disco could have been the assorted entrants for this year's Eurovision song contest. Holiday makers and locals all decked out in their finest fashion wear. It looked like an advert for Gullible Mug magazine. The junior brothers had congregated there too. This was what was causing the long queue. One by one an assortment of superheroes, furry animals and Mr Benn characters handed in their precious briefcases to the cloakroom.

Just behind them, Channella ,Leafetta and Camilla swigged on the bottle of champagne Camilla had picked up on her way past Happy Dolphin cottage. Leafetta could barely stand now, but she knew she'd pull it off when she had to make eye contact with the doormen, she always did.

At the back of the queue, refreshed from his kebab, was Monty. He could see some women up ahead, they all had some rather fetching leggings on he noticed.

His attention was sharply pulled away as a totally plastered Cowboy grabbed the front of Monty s jacket and slurred at him.

"Wheresh Tiger woman? I got plansh for her, I'm gonna gonna gonna make 'er very appy! I'm gonna make her purr alright!" And then his grip on Monty loosened and he slithered to his knees and repeated his last statement to the pavement before passing out.

Lowenna examined the contents of the wallet and quickly realised that something was badly amiss. The Client officer card for Troy's probation service appointments quickly told her that there was no doubt a file on Troy on the police computer. She only looked at the Royal mail ID card for a second and instantly recognised her cousin Dave. She knew how much Dave liked to forget his troubles in a lager mist on a Saturday afternoon. He might have dropped his wallet but looking at Troy's photo ID she felt fairly certain that Dave's belongings had ended up with the youth by a less innocent means.

She took out her phone and sent Dave a text. 'Have you lost your wallet Cuz? I have your driving licence, bank cards and ID, need to talk to you asap'

On the deck of a small fishing boat on the other side of the harbour, Dave's phone beeped in the dark.

Lowenna paused for a few moments trying to make up her mind whether to ring her cousin Jessica, Dave's wife. It was almost midnight now and Jessica was probably asleep. Lowenna thought about her uncomfortable visits to her cousin's house in the past.

It wasn't that they were blood relations which was the problem, lots of people married their first cousins around here. The most uncomfortable aspect was that Dave and Jessica lived their lives as if they couldn't stand one another. Dave refused to stop going to the Social club and so he regularly made use of the bed he'd build from old pallets in his garden shed.

Jessica on the other hand was intensely focused on self-development and personal growth.

Jessica had been extraordinarily successful with this approach to life. Once lean and trim, she had been experimenting with doughnuts and trifles and prosecco and had managed to develop her girth to the equivalent of a Nissan Micra. It was almost as if she was trying to model herself on some of the visitors.

Lowenna put her phone away, she'd pop up and see Dave in the morning, in the shed.

She tucked the wallet into her pocket and smiled as her cousin Raymond pulled up beside her in his taxi.

Inside the discotheque, the chaos at the cloakroom had now moved on to the bar. Most of the special club members were trying to get cheaper than bar price drinks. There was a lot of arm waving and hand clasping as the brothers attempted to make their special secret gestures and handshakes from beneath the fancy dress.

Camilla had managed to bypass all that nonsense by fluttering her false eyelashes at one of the bouncers, Derek Sprygelly. She reached out to his chest and ran her fingernails slowly from the top of his swollen pecs to his navel, allowing her hand to rest there for a few moments. "I get so anxious when I have to stand at a bar full of people" She looked up at him coyly "I know this isn't normal, but would you be allowed to go to the bar for me? I'd be ever so grateful" and then she added "We could go for a walk on the beach later if you like?"

Derek allowed the suggestion to filter through his consciousness. To anyone watching, it was like seeing an iceberg drift slowly across the horizon. "Uh, yeah, okay then" The muscle man had replied. She was a hot looking girl, and he could do with someone to come back to his flat and do the washing up. He probably wouldn't be able to do much with her because of all the steroids, but he could possibly get her to do a bit of hoovering.

Camilla handed him a £50 note and said, "We like champagne", Derek nodded. If she had money he thought, he could probably get her to pay for a Chinese later, and a taxi back to his place.

At the bar, Monty had finally been served. He'd been leaning over shouting "I was next" and waving a £20 note for ages. It had felt almost as if the bar staff were deliberately ignoring him. They had been. Only when Monty was the only one standing, and the glass washer had been emptied and the bar wiped down, did someone eventually serve him.

He spotted the trio he'd seen in the queue and headed over towards their table. He could see Channella and Leafettas faces, but the third girl had her back to him.

One of the doormen had just deposited a champagne bucket on the table. As he turned and walked away from the ladies, Derek made eye contact with Monty. For a second Derek looked Monty up and down approvingly, and then he winked at him.

Monty froze, poured his G&T down in one, and turned and went back to the bar. This time he just waited patiently without the note waving or vocal prompts. He was served a lot quicker.

Maurice unlocked his front door and placed his special briefcase on his kitchen table. Usually all he carried was his apron and a copy of Density and Spirit magazine. Maurice loved to read the horoscopes. Tonight, the case he had was much heavier and it made a satisfying thud as he deposited it. Maurice was happy. The visitors would be waking up to several new inconveniences and tonight's meeting had gone well.

The look on Alan's face had been priceless. Now he'd been enrolled, Alan would have no choice other than to help Maurice in making the two holiday apartments un-rentable. Once that was done, if Maurice were still there, he'd get Alan and Eileen to move out too. If he could just force the prices of the flats down enough, he could buy the building.

The mushroomed brothers had been hilarious to watch. It was a stunt he'd regularly employed back in the old town special hall. Maurice was impressed with the subliminal mind control Denzel had come up with too, so impressed he was planning on using the same CD manipulation technique on Denzel.
Maurice sniggered to himself

Maurice hadn't eaten or drunk much over the evening, but nature was calling now, and it would take a little while to peel off his morning suit and his sweaty rubber gear. Maurice looked at the clock. It was almost 1am. Soon it would be time to go out again, but not until he'd looked at all the money properly.

Just around the corner from Emmety Villa, the darkly dressed woman who'd been following Maurice climbed into her car and poured herself a cup of strong coffee from a flask. She knew he'd be out again once the streets were quiet. One a leopard, always a leopard.

She'd spent many nights like this before her career had ended. Usually she'd be teamed up with at least one, two or sometimes up to five more colleagues. Since she'd no longer been able to work in that field, she operated on her own.

She checked her phone. These days she ran a successful detective agency in Bristol. She'd made full use of all her contacts from her old job, and all the techniques she'd learned. There were three new messages but none of them were related to Maurice. She wasn't surprised, he always had been good at hiding what he was up to.

She shook her head as she remembered again her shock on the day his activities had been revealed. The chief superintendent had been sympathetic. He understood that she was in no way responsible, but clearly the best thing she could do, he'd suggested, was move somewhere far away and try to begin a new life. He'd even handed her an envelope of cash to help her on her way. It was from a few friends he'd said.

She'd decided not to move away and had used the generous wad of notes to find a new flat and to finance the opening of her agency.

What she really wanted to do was to find a way to get into Maurice's bank accounts and see just what he was living on, but that was impossible. She would just have to keep waiting and taking photos. She'd find a way to get to him eventually. She knew better than anyone that what Maurice really deserved, was to face justice.

In his shed, Dave snored oblivious to the cacophony of Saturday night sounds. Gull chicks made their high pitch squeaking noises. There were two boy racers revving their engines and burning around the main car park loudly. From the kebab shop came screaming and shouting as two women in their 50's slogged it out in front of a fascinated crowd. Up Shutta Lane a drunk woke residents with an imaginative but not quite lyrically complete rendition of Sweet Caroline. An assortment of dogs joined in with their approval. From the seafront a selection of younger voices woohooed and made ape noises loudly in the darkness.

The mayor was listening to all this from the privacy of his back lawn. He'd been home for a couple of hours now and his friends from CID had assured him there would be no record of the evening's earlier incident.

He reflected on just how much the sounds echoed around the valley. The town had always been like this, it was rarely quiet, even at 3am. He extinguished the joint he'd been smoking and went in to bed.

Damien was dreaming. He was tearing along the straight at Silverstone. His Seat Ibiza was especially loud, he felt proud.

In the room next door, River and Ocean were dreaming of ice cream buffets and toy shops and the satisfying sound of amplifiers exploding.

Downstairs, Troy was dreaming too. He was tearing along the straight at Silverstone. His Seat Ibiza was especially loud, he felt proud.

Veryan and Mike shuffled in bed trying to get comfortable. Veryan turned to face away from Mike who was on his back and beginning to make the snuffling sounds which usually preceded his deafening throaty snorts. Veryan knew she'd probably end up in the spare room again. It wasn't that she didn't want to be close to Mike, but there was nothing in the least bit romantic about two people trying to get to sleep on a soft platform just four-foot six wide. No wonder the divorce rate was so high she thought to herself as she tugged the quilt back over to her side.

Lowenna was doing a little better. She and her husband had decided several years ago that single beds meant better sleep for both and a far happier relationship. As time had moved on and the children had gone, they'd taken down one of the partition walls to enlarge their bedroom. Now they both slept blissfully each with their own double bed.

Uncle Keith had come to in a cell. He didn't remember how he'd arrived there.

Outside the kebab shop, a police car had

arrived and split the two women up. The disappointed crowd had gradually begun to disperse.

In the discotheque, the brothers were strutting their finest moves. Monty looked at the bizarre mixture of outfits and then caught Derek watching him from a corner, Derek winked again.

Monty looked away quickly and asked for a bottle of fizz from the bar. It was time to join the three girls in the spectacular leggings. Two of them were dancing now. Leafetta was asleep on the table. Monty still hadn't seen the face of the third girl, but he was thoroughly impressed with the way she wiggled, if only Camilla could move like that he thought. "That'll be £35 mate" Monty handed the barman a fifty. He picked up the bottle and his change and began to approach the tiger stripes and leopard prints.

Just then, Camilla turned and they made eye contact. For a second it was as if everything else in the room had frozen. Monty was stunned, Camilla had never looked this good, but beside that he puzzled, what an earth was she doing in here?

Camilla swore under her breath, she'd forgotten to keep track of Monty once they'd left the Galleon. She recovered with the speed of a private school girl just as she'd been taught. "Oh great" she greeted Monty, "I'm glad you found it, you must have found my note?" Camilla reminded herself to scribble a quick note when she went to the ladies. She could plant it in the cottage when she got back.

She stepped forward to kiss Monty and spotted the cheap prosecco he was holding
"Oh well done lover, you think of everything"
Monty was confused but decided to play along. Before he could take another step, from the edge of the dance floor, Darth Vader stumbled into Monty and sent him careering into a table which he upset spilling all the drinks. The now drink-less drinkers were on their feet in a thrice. Monty was confronted with five angry faces.

Derek looked on. This was a tricky one. Really, he should throw Darth Vader out of the club. Unfortunately he knew from the briefcases in the cloakroom that Darth Vader and all his chums were probably 'brothers'. Derek knew better than to mess with members of the special club.

The bloke holding the prosecco was cute he thought, but if he played along with the woman in the tiger prints, Camilla, he might just get his kitchen cleaned. He decided to stand back and see what happened next rather than wade in.

Derek saw the head doorman looking at him from the exits door, on his ear piece Derek heard his boss tell him "Just have a word with him eh? Tell who ever it is inside that ridiculous outfit to calm down"

Derek crossed the room. He tapped on Darth Vader's shoulder.

"I need to talk to you mate"

Darth turned.

"Ah, Derek, I see you're working tonight then" Darth answered. The special filter in the mask making the voice sound just it did in the films. Derek was a little taken aback.

"How did Do you know my name? "

Darth Vader was taking his headpiece off.
Derek was the one who was shocked now,
"I am your father Derek"

Derek watched his dad apologise to everyone,
he was quickly joined by Princess Leia.
who set about pacifying the occupants of the
upset table and then headed promptly toward
the bar to replace all the drinks. Derek
whispered a silent prayer that Princess Leia
wasn't his mum. He could only see the back of
the outfit. Princess Leia turned, Derek wasn't
sure whether to feel relieved or horrified,
Princess Leia was his uncle Jonathan.

Back in the Old Gaol, Alan, still dressed as the
Wizard, had finished talking to the fire
extinguisher about his plans for the future. He'd
also had to explain that he wasn't a real wizard,
but he hoped to be one day. The fire
extinguisher had made some interesting points
and had some really good ideas. Denzel was
tapping Alan on the shoulder now though so it

was time to say goodnight.

"Come on matey, it's time to get you home."

Alan hadn't had the same programming the rest of the brothers had been subjected to and turned to Denzel slowly. He still felt buzzy from the mushrooms, he liked it. "That was bloody fabulous punch, what was in it?" He asked. It slowly dawned on Alan that everyone else had gone now. "Oh!" he said, "Where's everyone else?"

"Some have gone home and everyone else went to the disco" Denzel answered.

Alan thought the disco sounded like a great idea. Since he'd been 22, it had seemed like a great idea about once a year when he'd been out with friends and had two or three too many. On every occasion, he'd regretted it afterwards for months, swearing he would never set foot in that terrible place again. He was torn. Denzel took charge. He'd assured Maurice he would see Alan home and he wasn't going to fail in his obligations.
"It's late Alan, how about I pick up a bottle of

Brandy from my shop and we can have a late drink? I'll drop you off f you like"

Alan thought he'd rather be seen dead than spotted riding shotgun in Denzel's yellow Jaguar. He fumbled his words. "Would it be okay if I got changed at home then?" He'd decided he really liked the wizard outfit and if he kept the hat pulled down, even if they did drive past someone he knew, no one ought to recognise him.

Denzel agreed. They gathered their belongings. As they did to Alan embarrassment the tub of Vaseline fell from his trouser pocket and hit the floor with a loud thunk.
Denzel looked across the room at Alan questioningly. "I wasn't sure what was going to happen" Alan blurted.
Denzel Nodded knowingly and offered Alan reassurance "I completely understand, can't be too prepared and all that" Alan was relaxing and then Denzel added "Tonight was the initiation, you won't need the Vaseline until *next* week" and then he quickly turned away to hide the grin he was wearing.

Camilla had nipped out to the loo. Monty was clearly rather taken with Channella, and Camilla had quite liked the look of Damien. The other one, the one who'd had his knackers crunched was grubby, and although a lot younger than Cowboy, he was just the type Camilla usually liked to stalk for her 'no strings' brief encounters. There was clearly some potential here she thought.

Leafetta had woken from her slumber, downed a pint of lager in one and then gone back to sleep on the table. Camilla was about to go back towards the dance floor when she remembered the note. She paused by a sink to scribble a few words on an envelope she had in her handbag.

WOKE UP TO FIND YOU'D GONE OUT
YOU CAN'T BE FAR AWAY
I'VE COME TO LOOK FOR YOU
IF YOU GET IN BEFORE ME, DON'T WORRY ABOUT ME,
EVEN IF I'M LATE BACK
LOVE YOU, CAMMYKINS XXXXX

She could leave that somewhere in the cottage

when they got back.

Monty was dancing with Channella now. He wasn't her usual type and she and Damien were married of course, but Damien wasn't there and what he didn't know wouldn't hurt him. Camilla wasn't back from the toilet yet, Channella had seen the huge queue for the ladies. The disco held about 600 people but there were only 3 cubicles in the ladies and one of those had no pot in it. Channella reckoned Camilla would be gone for a little longer yet.

She took Monty by the hand and led him to a corner where an Oompa Loompa and Austin Powers were giving their al to 'Does your mother know' concealing them from everyone else. She gently pulled Monty towards her and pushed her tongue through his lips and began working it like a camel searching for chewing gum.
Monty was delighted, but a little surprised by the force and dexterity of her tongue, his alert radar was working on full now and he knew Camilla wasn't far away. A loud voice intruded

"Well, yourz not tiger woman, but you'll do" Out

of nowhere, Cowboy had appeared. The snogging stopped and they turned to face the scruffy builder.

"Ello gorgeous, wanna come dan the beech wiv me? I've already got rubbers....if I ken find 'em"

Both Channella and Monty were speechless, and then over Cowboys shoulder, Channella spotted Camilla coming back through the main doors. In the dark lights of the disco, Camilla didn't recognise Cowboy.

Camilla spotted Monty and her new friend talking to a rough looking pensioner and nodded to them to let them know she was there. Channella nodded back in acknowledgement.

Cowboy, assuming the nod had been in response to his generous offer tried to grab Channella's hand. "Come on then love" he leered at her.

Monty found his voice

"Oi! Just a minute"

Cowboy placed his hand on Monty's chest and shoved hard. Years of lifting and carrying bricks and bags of plaster had made his muscles as strong as the concrete he'd buried his last wife in. "Piss orf you little squirt" he told Monty "She's mine naa!"

Austin Powers had been quick to react and caught the rather surprised Monty before he could go crashing into anyone or anything. At that point, luckily for everyone another loud voice entered the arena. She only said one word but the affect was stunning "COWBOY!" Cowboy released Channella's reluctant hand "Aw feck" he uttered, and turned slowly so he was face to face with his girlfriend.

She was called Doris. In her long career as a police Sargent in Bristol, she'd had to deal with all sorts of situations. Some were simply poorly thought out drunken antics, some were vicious, some were spontaneous and some had been well planned and executed.
Maurice had fallen into the last group.

Doris knew the full depth of Maurice's manipulations. He had embezzled large sums of money to finance his perversions. He'd also manipulated his fellow brothers in the 'Special club' he'd belonged to before he'd moved to the little seaside town.

He'd made full use of his contacts to take over the Manor House in the Hartcliffe district of Bristol.

He'd chosen well, it was the last place anyone would have thought to look for him and his ill-gotten gains. The steel shutters on the doors and windows were normal in that part of town, as were the barbed wire and death threat trespasser warning notices.

No one would have guessed what a contrast was hidden inside.

He'd filled it with velvet and silk and mirrors. When Doris had gone to see the place for herself, it had looked like something from the Arabian nights, an enormous luxurious harem. It wasn't populated with people though, it was full of manikins, each one dressed in a different set of frillies. Maurice had set up cameras throughout.

The officers who viewed the footage of Maurice dancing to his favourite tunes while bedecked in women's underwear, had to receive months of counselling afterwards.

One of the most disturbing features was that Maurice had commissioned the manikins especially from a manufacturer in the far east and although the bodies were female, the faces were all clearly Maurice's very own.

Maurice had embezzled hundreds of thousands of pounds to finance his passion and had well paid security patrolling the site.

When it came to his choice in underwear, Maurice bought from the finest suppliers he could find. There wasn't a single pair of C&A knickers in the place. They just weren't good enough for Maurice back then. He required hand stitched silk and the finest Italian satins. He had stolen, cheated, defrauded, embezzled and burgled to realise his dream.

Doris was one of the people he'd ruined. She hadn't known there was a problem until she came home one day to discover the locks on her house had been changed. County Court Bailiffs had repossessed the building for the mortgage company.

It didn't take the heartbroken Doris long to figure out whose work had led to that. She'd taken a leave from work and followed him until she'd discovered his lair.

The case had never made it to court. Many of the brothers were too embarrassed, several were desperate that their own financial affairs didn't come under any scrutiny.
The chief superintendent certainly didn't want any publicity that money recovered from drugs dealers by his force had been taken and used. These were just the tip of a very large iceberg.

Disgusted, Doris had left the force. Maurice had disappeared. It had taken her four years to find him. He'd kept his first name, but she knew now he'd switched his middle and last names. Now he was Maurice Thomas John.

She'd found him quite by chance when she'd bumped into an old school friend who'd known them both.

As they chatted over their supermarket trolleys the friend, who knew nothing about what had transpired said "You'll never guess who I saw

when I was in Cornwall a couple of weeks
ago?"
Doris had booked a place on a campsite, put
her work on hold, and had driven down the next
day.
She'd been following him for a week now, and
he had no idea whatsoever that he was being
carefully watched.

Doris was still sipping coffee when a ridiculous
looking Jaguar pulled around the corner. Who
on earth would want a banana yellow one she
wondered? The driver had been smartly
dressed in what looked like a morning suit.
Doris decided he must be a special club
member. The passenger reminded her of the
episode with the Wizard in Mr Benn. Doris used
to love watching Mr Benn. She decided to have
a closer look.

Denzel was walking up the steps to Emmety
Villa. Alan unsurprisingly, seemed a little
unsteady. He was almost incoherent now. Doris
wondered if they had anything to do with
Maurice but then an upstairs light came on in
the building. A few minutes later having left
Alan on his sofa, Denzel came back down the

stairs and drove off.

Doris watched Denzel for just long enough to miss Maurice's skinny figure slip out of a side door, hop over the garden fence into the garden next door, and then head up the lane towards Sunrising. He knew he was taking a risk by going out so early, but he just couldn't help himself. The desire to acquire some new underwear was overwhelming.

In the disco the lights had come on and the glasses were being cleared away. Channella had given Monty and Camilla her phone number and they'd arranged to meet up the following day. They hadn't known what to do with Leafetta, she wouldn't wake up and she was far too heavy to carry. They left her where she was and walked to the taxi rank. Monty stopped in a shop doorway to urinate. Now he was out of earshot Camilla said to Channella "What do you think about these couples who swap partners when they're on holiday?"

Channella couldn't believe her ears, she wondered if there really was a god and he'd heard her thoughts earlier. "I think if the bloke

looked like your Monty, I would" she gave Camilla a wink and a nudge. Camilla didn't waste a second. "Interesting, do you think your Damien would feel the same?"
"Oh I reckon he would, he would if it was you anyway" She added "I know he plays away sometimes when he goes off to football, but then, I've got my own little secrets too" in the back of her mind, Channella wondered if she'd reordered her regular prescription from the special clinic.

Camilla took Channella's hands in her own, "shall we then?" Camilla decided to go the whole way "I quite fancied that Troy too, shame he had to go so early"
"I liked him too" Channella confessed "Perhaps tomorrow we could all work something out?" Camilla nodded and smiled. Monty re-joined them. He reached out his hand to take Camilla's, it was wet.

Channella spotted a taxi and began frantically waving at the driver. Emmety Villa was at least a five-minute walk. Unless she was shopping or going on the raz, Channella hated walking. She said goodnight and gave Monty a peck on the cheek and a wink. Camilla and Monty set off back for Happy Dolphin Cottage. Camilla explained that tomorrow, they'd be having a little partner swapping fun. Monty didn't know what to say when Camilla had finished, what if he ended up with the one they'd left asleep in the disco? He felt a small shudder go down his spine.

Denzel pulled up by the kerb outside his house and climbed out of the bananmobile. He had plenty of room on the drive but he liked everyone to be able to see his car.

He unlocked the front door, turned off the alarm and went to drop his keys on the ghastly shabby chic regency table. The table was authentic, he'd paid £12000 for it at auction. One of his nieces had persuaded him that Shabby chic was the way forward and the table was now wearing a covering of his favourite colour chalk paint. It had been hard to get yellow chalk paint, and ridiculously expensive, but Denzel was a man who appreciated fine things so he felt it had been worthwhile.

On the table was a small box "Bugger!" Denzel

exclaimed as he realised he'd forgotten.
The box contained a gold-plated hip flask
Denzel had bought and had engraved
especially for Maurice. Denzel planned to be
number two at the special club soon, and he
knew only too well the value of a little grooming.
He decided he could drop it off tomorrow when
he went to visit Alan, or more importantly,
Eileen. He must get his briefcase back too.
He'd given Maurice the money in it, but the
case hadn't been part of the deal. It had been a
present from his mum when Denzel had first
gone to Camborne college and it had a small
brass plaque on top with his name on it. He
made a mental note to pick it up the following
day after he'd done the weekly sacking.

Denzel liked to sack people, but not family of
course. It kept everyone else on their toes.
He would interview people knowing secretly
that he could ditch them in a week or at least
before the end of their probationary period. It
meant Denzel could constantly pay low wages
and he rarely got involved with anything like
employment contracts. If Mark Wray, the
employment compliance officer had known,
he'd have hauled Denzel into his office in a

thrice. Denzel made sure that Mark was kept busy elsewhere.

He was going to sack Katrina in the morning. Katrina had come from Poland a few years ago and worked like a trojan. Denzel rented her and her boyfriend a small flat. He would sack Katrina and then get the boyfriend to work on his garden for a pittance. He'd have to do it, or Denzel would throw them out of the flat. He'd offer Katrina her old job back once his garden was finished, but at a lower rate of pay.

He dressed in his yellow silk pyjamas and slide into his super super super king size bed between his yellow silk sheets. He was asleep within seconds.

At last the assorted brothers all had the correct briefcases. Most of them stumbled back to their cars. There were several crunches as inebriated special club members attempted to navigate out of the car park. A few joined the queue at the kebab shop. The one dressed as a chef got as far as the front door of his restaurant and crumpled into an unconscious heap in the porch. Count Dracula went back to his under takers shop and got his head down inside one of his demonstration caskets which was conveniently displayed in the window.

One of the taxi drivers had spotted the fancy dressed figures and particularly the briefcases. He got on the radio to his fellows, "Pass the word, the dodgy trouser brigade are at it again" was all he said. The other drivers would know exactly what that meant. In a town of so many fraternities and committees, things like this happened with an alarming frequency. He put down his radio. If he'd seen an ordinary drunk driver, he would probably have rung 101, there was no point with this lot though, they could do whatever they liked. They owned the town.

At last the car park was quiet again and the taxis went back to ferrying drunk people back to wherever they were going to spend the night. Raymond returned from his break after taking Lowenna home. His first fare was a married couple who seemed intent on eating one another as he drove them to Sunrising. Just a normal Saturday night he thought to himself. He had to ask where they were going. He knew them both and where they lived, the difficulty was they weren't married to each other.

On his way past the shops, Raymond noticed Darth Vader and Austin Powers stumbling along the pavement. A little further on spotted a darkly dressed figure. He knew instantly it was that creepy bloke from Emmety Villa. The one who liked to moan about the toilets and the visitors as if he'd been here all his life.

The taxis drivers didn't gossip and they didn't discuss all the things they saw, but between them there wasn't a thing that happened in the town they didn't know about. Raymond wondered if he ought to mention to cousin Lowenna that he thought creepy Maurice was their knickers thief.
He'd give it some thought.

Virtually all the punters had gone, only the staff remained in the discotheque now, and Leafetta. She was just beginning to stir. Paul the head doorman motioned for Derek to stay for locking up and sent the rest of his crew home.
"Hahahaha, fancy that being your old man, shall we call you Luke from now on?" he cajoled Derek.

Derek was over the shock now "My family are so embarrassing he replied shaking his head but grinning"
"You know what Derek, all families are embarrassing" They laughed.

Paul gestured towards Leafetta "Your turn or mine?"
Derek knew it was his turn. Dealing with incapacitated punters was the job and most nights at least one person managed to render themselves incapable of finding their own way home. If the punter was in danger it meant an ambulance, if they were drunk and burbling as most of them were, in the summer the bouncers would wait until the street was quiet and then manhandle them down to the seafront to sleep it off.

They couldn't get any sense out of Leafetta and they knew none of the taxi drivers would allow her in their cars like that. It looked like the seafront was going to be her final destination. Paul left to begin checking everything was properly locked while Derek managed to get Leafetta to her uncooperative feet and make a start towards the exit.

Leafetta, feeling herself being moved was beginning to come round.

"Oo you're gorduze" she slurred and swung her other arm up so that she was hanging off Derek's neck.
"God help me" muttered Derek; this one was going to take a while.

The town clock struck twice, the few people still awake to hear it knew it was 3am. Gradually the trickle of drunks reduced, and taxis picked up their last fares for the evening. The town always sported a few unusual offerings for anyone patient enough to look at that time of the morning.
Derek said goodnight to his friends at the Chinese takeaway and headed home. There were various items of clothing deposited around the town, either lost by drunks or dropped from pushchairs. He counted two single trainers and a single men's size 9 Croc. In the doorway of the Pirate restaurant the chef looked as if he'd decided to spend the night there and was snoring loudly. A little further down the road a cat stalked the constantly active gulls. The windows were open in the flat above the tackle shop and the heavy aroma of home-grown

weed floated down to the street. Just like his cousin Raymond, Derek thought to himself, just another normal Saturday night.

Derek took all this in as he absently wondered if he could get mum round to clean his flat. It was a shame about Tiger girl but he'd have felt bad when he had to show her the door after she'd finished washing up, he always did.

The girl with the Green Army tattoo who'd stayed had been a nightmare. Just as he was hauling her out through the door she'd begun shouting.
"Idon'twannagohomeyet. Iwannanotherdrink".
She'd kept on and on and on. In the end he'd dropped her on the steps and grabbed a bottle of cheap cider they kept in the kitchen to feed the cook when he was under pressure.

Once he'd managed to get Leafetta to focus on that, things had become a lot easier. He'd left her on a bench outside Denzel's Plaice promising he'd come back shortly, and he would, but probably not until tomorrow afternoon.

"Bringusbackanotherbottledarlin" Leafetta has slurred.

Doris waited and watched. There was still a light on in Maurice's flat. Doris had learned to be patient; she knew she'd spot him eventually. She watched as Channella arrived back at the apartment. Even after her vast experience, Channella's leggings were quite shocking. The leopard print and skin tone made her look as if she were naked but blotchy. Doris made a lightning fast assessment and decided to check on the registration numbers of the other vehicles parked outside Emmety Villa. Perhaps Maurice was running some sort of agency?

Meanwhile, Maurice was finishing his circuit of one of the estates that overlooked a little beach. The houses were more expensive here, and so were the undies that got left out to dry on these warm summer evenings. He'd been successful. Crammed into the pockets of his dark tracksuit were two brassieres and three pairs of knickers. He'd also pocketed a couple of pairs of Marks and Spencer fluorescent green trimmed Y fronts that looked like his size.

Twice he'd had to duck out of the lights of first a

taxi and then a roaming police car. That was all part of the excitement though, and Maurice could be pretty quick on his toes when he needed too.

He would have gone out every night if he could such was his hunger for more silk and nylon treasure. It was just too risky though. Maurice struggled. He got through underwear the way people got through beer. Sometimes he'd binge and wear 7 or 8 different sets in a session. He always kept everything, but Maurice liked to have a constantly fresh supply. He'd read all about heroin addiction, alcoholism, cigarettes and compulsive eating and he knew that his commitment to satisfying his urges went far beyond any of those activities.

Maurice was off to visit the street where the Mayor lived now. The Mayors wife had left the town with another woman just a few months ago and the Mayor had similar interests to Maurice, it was just that he fulfilled his needs by post.

Maurice had learned this quite by chance. He'd been trying to recruit the Mayor into the special club for ages. He'd called up at the house on several occasions and last time, he'd gone with a big bottle of Lambrusco. They'd sat in the very private back garden. Obviously, his host had forgotten what was hanging on the drier. Maurice suspected that on a warm night like this, he might well find something to fit him on that road. What he was really hoping for were some suspender belts. In an age of hold ups, they were getting harder to find, but Maurice rather fancied he'd get lucky when he got to number 13.

All over the town the noise level finally reduced until it was less of a cacophony and more of a lullaby. Gulls squawked, the breeze made barely a murmur and the waves lapped peacefully at the shoreline. Outside the fish and chip shop, a group of fishermen who'd given up casting from the pier, stopped to admire Leafetta. She mumbled in her sleep "Jusonemorefertheroadpleesh" They posed beside her while they took it in turns to immortalise the moment on their phones.

There was a small drama unfolding in the supermarket. The three-man night fill crew had been joined by a new recruit. Things had been going well and they'd worked together to fill up the freezers and the pet food. The tinned food aisle was next on the list and the new lad, Justin, was working well. It had all gone wrong when he'd moved onto the home baking section. Dave, David and Davy had gone to the rear doors to let the milk and newspapers deliveries in.

They'd heard a blood curdling scream from the shop floor and then Justin had come running out to the back door carrying a pack of flour screaming "I hate you! I hate you!"

He'd torn the outer cellophane open and now he was hurling bags of flour into the street "Get out" he shouted, and "You can go do one!" as he hurled another.

Dave tried to calm him "Steady on mate, what's the problem?"

David joined the confusion as an airborne bag almost hit the milk delivery driver in the chest. "Justin, dude? Are you okay?"

Davy came from the fridge where he'd been storing the following days milk.

"Oh god, we were warned this might happen"

"What?" said both Dave and David in harmony.

"Well after the interview, his mum rang us to warn us"

"I can't bloody stand you!" shouted Justin as he launched another packet.

"What?" said both Dave and David in harmony again.

"He's gluten intolerant" Davy explained.

Maurice came back out from the mayors garden a lot faster than he'd gone in. He didn't know the neighbours had a dog and the bloody thing had begun to bark loudly. A few seconds later a security light had come on nearly blinding Maurice, he vacated the scene in a panic and scrambled over a fence into the back of the old petrol station. His heart was pounding and worse still, the line had been barren.

He continued along the road until he came to the alleyway which led to the backs of another stretch of houses, perhaps he would find something here he thought.

He reached into his pocket for his earlier finds to reassure himself and discovered to his huge disappointment that he only had the y fronts now. He must have lost the other items when he'd scrambled over the fence and climbed over the half dozen abandoned cars. He swore to himself.

If he could embezzle enough money from the brotherhood, he could go back to purchasing the way he used to, but Maurice was short on funds and anyway, knowing things had been worn already was a apart of the thrill for him.

His circuit of the retirement bungalows turned out to be as disappointing as his visit to the Mayors house. Not a pair of apple catchers anywhere. A fat tabby cat hissed at Maurice from a fence top. Maurice hissed back.

Doris checked the time and realised something was wrong. She'd gone carefully up the long flight of steps to Emmety Villa. There was little illumination as Maurice liked to turn off the external lights when there were visitors in the building. Doris listened but the only noises coming from downstairs were those of someone snoring loudly. She knew it wasn't

Maurice, she'd have recognised his unique tones if it had been. She took a chance and peeked into one of the windows.

She could see into the bedroom. He wasn't there. The wardrobe doors were open. Maurice was definitely still maintaining his hobby.

The bedroom door was ajar and hanging from a hook on the back was something that resembled a wet suit. This item wasn't intended to be worn at any beach though, Doris almost sniggered but then the memory of how badly she'd been wronged came flooding back so she gritted her teeth and continued.

Doris kept her back to the wall and sidled along to the next window. This turned out to be the lounge. The blinds were partially open. Just inside and between the back of the sofa and the window was a clothes airer, it held an assorted collection of undergarments, all women's. The lounge door was wide open and was directly opposite the kitchen. Maurice wasn't there either. On the kitchen table was a briefcase, the same one Maurice had brought home with him earlier. It had looked heavy.

Maurice was either asleep in the lavatory or he'd slipped out another way.

Doris moved along the wall and then up the few short steps to Maurice's front door. She quietly lifted the letter box flap and peered in. The hallway contained the assortment of tacky items Doris had learned to expect from Maurice. In one corner there was a plastic model of a well with two facsimiles of a mother and calf elephant. There were foil elephant pictures on the walls and all around the skirting and on the Formica hall table were a dazzling assortment of wooden, plastic and china elephants, not one of them realistic and not one of them tastefully done.

Doors led off the hallway into the rooms she'd already looked at. At the end of the hallway was a door marked FIRE EXIT.

"Dammit!" she said quietly to herself "The git must have stolen out of that one"

That meant he could come back at any time. She hurried back to the windows she'd already visited and took a few photos of each room quickly. She put her special camera back inside her jacket and hurried back down the steps to her car.

In the town centre, the four fishermen had been slowly walking while they chatted about the history of the town and some of the places which were said to be haunted. They were just walking past the supermarket when out of nowhere, a bag of flour hit one of them straight on the ear sending him staggering towards the window opposite. As he tried to maintain his balance, he lifted his hands to brace himself on the shop window. He recoiled abruptly as Dracula sat up in his coffin and rubbed his eyes. The floured man let out a scream so loud that in the different parts of town, both Doris and Maurice heard it.

Maurice was covering the ground quickly now. In about an hour it would begin to get light again. Maurice definitely preferred darkness. He was beginning to get anxious. He thought about going back to the garage, but he felt that surly he'd find something. The search continued.

Like a fox looking for dustbins, Maurice seemed to skip through the night visiting paths and alley ways and rear entrances. Still nothing. He came to the house on the corner with a big neighbourhood watch sticker in the front window. This was Lowenna's house. As he glanced down the path alongside the house, he could see garments hanging from the long line which ran down the back garden to the bank where the field began.

"No way" he told himself "It's just too risky". The urge was almost overwhelming, but Maurice managed to overcome it, and he carried on down the hill in the direction he'd been heading.

Leafetta had woken up. She'd been dreaming about chips. A loud scream had broken though her consciousness. She pulled herself upright and noticed the half full cider bottle Derek had left her clutching. by a miracle, it was still in her lap. "waste not want not" she said to no one in particular and unscrewed to the top. Before she could take a swig, she realised that she was bursting for a wee. She heard the town clock strike three times as she shuffled over to the doorway of Denzel's to relieve herself.

Troy would have been proud of her. As she balanced and emptied, with her other hand, she topped up again. She tossed the empty bottle into the corner with her puddle and set off back towards Emmety Villa trying to remember what had happened. Whatever it was she thought, it must have been an amazing night.

Maurice was getting frantic, he'd heard the three stokes and knew that even on a Sunday, there were still some unfortunate souls who rose at 4 am to go to their daily grind, especially if they worked for Denzel. He had to move quickly, it would be light in half an hour, he was running out of time.

He almost started crying when he got to the end of the route he'd planned that morning. All that effort and nothing but two pairs of Y fronts. Maurice was angry and frustrated. His judgement was becoming severely clouded. He came to the end of the last section of his 'patrol' as he liked to think of it.
Nothing.
He sank to his knees on a grass verge and lifted his head to implore heaven. "Why won't you help me?" His voice was shaky. Then he

remembered the house on the corner. If he was quick, and he could be surprisingly quick for a man of his age when the need arose, he could make it.

Lowenna was awake. Despite the separate beds, her husband would wake when it got light every morning and tiptoe out to the bathroom. He'd be as quiet as he could but Lowenna always woke up then too. She waited for him to finish so she could take her turn in the throne room.

Maurice felt inside his tracksuit. He still had his rubber balaclava in the inside pocket. He tugged it over his head. Ordinarily it would have tugged his hair, but Maurice was sweating heavily now as the adrenaline rushed around his body. The intense darkness of night had passed quickly and the sky to the east was getting lighter at an alarming rate. He fiddled to correctly align the eye holes and the stepped out from behind the large pampas grass in Lowenna's front garden.
He glanced up at the windows and then dashed towards the path that he hoped would lead to

treasure. There was no time to lose, if Lowenna
was on early turn she could open the curtains
at any minute. He thought about giving up for
the night but the compulsion to view the line
was in full control of Maurice now. He stepped
forward into the back garden.

Lowenna sat and released her night wind. In
the bedroom as he always did, her husband
laughed at the amplified volley.
Maurice worked quickly down the washing line.
There was a cardigan, two pairs of trousers,
two white blouses with Lowenna's insignia on
them. As Maurice stepped forward with his
eyes fixed on the line, his foot came down on
something smooth and at a different level from
the path. He felt his foot slip under him and for
a moment was completely airborne before he
came thumping down onto the dew moistened
lawn.
Lowenna pulled the flush and thought she
heard a strange wet thumping sound. It was
probably the plumbing.

Maurice recovered quickly and was back on his
feet in an instant. For a second, he pulled back
his foot to kick the cement tortoise he'd stepped

on and then decided better of it. He carried on swiftly down the line. Another cardigan, some vests, half a dozen tea towels. He was almost at the end of the line now. On the very end hung a bathmat and a pair of large bath towels. "Noooooooooo" Maurice bunched his fists and suppressed his angst between gritted teeth. He knew he'd better get out of there quickly.

As he turned, he spotted like Excalibur rising from the lake, the rotary drier by the back door. And it was loaded.

Lowenna was just leaving the bathroom when she heard the rotary drier make its customary high pitched squeak . She stepped swiftly towards the landing window just in time to see a tall skinny man in a tracksuit and rubber balaclava reaching towards her laundry.

" OI!" she shouted as she fumbled to open the window. "You stop right there"

Maurice snatched at the line and plucked off two pairs of Lowenna's best. He dashed up the path towards the front door and just as Lowenna threw it open, smartly changed direction and went hurtling down back down the garden path. Benny Hill would have been proud.

Before Lowenna had made it halfway down the garden, Maurice had run up the practically vertical grass covered bank and thrown himself over the top. Maurice landed in a tangle of brambles and nettles on the other side. He rolled away from the vicious thorns onto the freshly ploughed soil. With the grace of a three-legged hippo, he was back on his feet in a thrice. He could hear Lowennas footsteps on the path as she ran to follow him. He ran a few yards down the field and then stepped back into the brambles as he threw himself back over the bank and into another garden. By the time Lowenna had clambered to the top of the bank, Maurice was partway through the garden. He dashed out onto the pavement, took a sharp right hand turn and fled towards the bottom of the estate and safe passage home.

Maurice had only travelled a few more yards when he narrowly avoided colliding with Lowenna and Veryans Nana.
A lifelong early riser, she was out for her first

walk of the day with Brian, her cocker spaniel.
Nana looked on in utter shock as a freshly
muddy rubber headed creature loomed out of
nowhere. As she braced for impact, the mud
creature dived to the left to pass her, and then
went careering on down the hill. She shook her
head. If one thing in life was certain, you saw
some strange sites in this town.
Brian, completely absorbed in his own
activities, just carried on sniffing at fence
bottoms.

Nana quickly collected herself from the surprise
and carried on up the road. She'd gone another
hundred yards when Lowenna, dressed just in
a nightie came hobbling down the road towards
her.

"Did you see him?" Lowenna gasped.
"Oh hello love, what on earth are you doing
working in your nightie? Why haven't you got
anything on your feet?" and then seeing the
pained look on Lowennas face "He went that
way love, I have to say, he's pretty fast
whoever he is"
Lowenna had decided the pursuit was
pointless. "Did you see his face Nana?"

Nana shock her head slowly "No love" she answered "and from what he was wearing, I hope I never do"

As Leafetta approached the supermarket, she saw Dave and David outside in the street attempting to sweep up a mess of flour and torn flour bags. Davy say beside the now subdued Justin on the back doorstep trying to console the clearly upset youth.

Leafetta felt inside her pocket and was delighted to discover she still had her purse. It was full of the money she'd lifted from that bloke last night. She remembered that bit quite clearly.

She turned into the small alleyway beside the shop and tried to step over Davy and Justin. "Excuse me" said Davy loudly "what do you think you're doing?"
Leafetta looked puzzled "I'm hungry" she answered "I want food, you're open aren't you?"
Dave and David had come back to into the alleyway now. Dave offered
"It's ten past four on Sunday morning, does it look like were open?"
Leafetta thought about it.

"Well you look like you're open. Shouldn't you be working rather than playing food fights?" David had had enough, he encountered enough difficult emmets during his day job in one of Denzel's fudge shops.

"Well we aren't, so piss off"

Leafetta was stunned. She was used to talking to other people like that, but she certainly wasn't accustomed to anyone reciprocating.

"You can't speak to me like that. I want to see the manager" In classic pose she placed her hands on her hips and stamped her foot as reinforcement.

Even Justin joined in the laughter that followed.

Maurice cut off from the footpath and headed into the trees. The wood ran along the side of the valley and behind the top of the garden at Seaview. He pulled off his balaclava and stuffed it back in his pocket. If anyone did see him emerging from the woods and question him, he could explain that he'd been early morning badger watching.

A smile crossed his face. When American films had introduced the term beaver in reference to female anatomy, Maurice had insisted that in

Britain we ought to use the term Badger. The word had taken on a whole new meaning.

He was almost home now. He made his way through a gap in the fence and stepped back onto the safe soil of Seaview.

Doris had been watching Leafetta wobble the steps of Seaview. The skin tone leggings had picked up an unfortunate stain while Leafetta had slumbered on the bench outside Denzel's place. It wasn't a good look.

Above the sound of the gulls wheeling and chanting in the new day, Doris's well-trained ears could hear movement in the bushes at the top of the garden. Twigs and branches were being snapped by something heavy.

She ducked behind Troy's Corsa and peeked up just in time to see the mud-covered figure she'd been stalking emerge from the wood. She whipped her special camera from her pocket and began to photograph her prey.

Maurice was still running on adrenaline. He worked his way quickly down the garden and towards his front door. He paused by an ornamental plastic swan to retrieve his spare keys. As he stood up again, he didn't notice that his balaclava had slipped from his pocket. From her vantage point, Doris continued to take photographs until the door closed behind him.

Once inside, Maurice went straight to the bathroom where he relieved himself and stripped off before climbing into the shower. When he finished drying himself, he donned his threadbare and stained dressing gown.

He scooped up his tracksuit and felt in the pocket for his prizes. He felt a familiar thrill as his fingers made contact with the material of Lowenna robust and practical poly cottons. He glanced at them for a moment and then transferred them to the pocket of his grubby robe.
Dumping his other garments in the laundry basket, he paused briefly in the kitchen. He closed the blind and then opened the briefcase Denzel had given him. He gazed in satisfaction at the bundles of £20 notes.

It was almost 5am now, and Maurice was yawning. What a night it had been. Leaving the open briefcase on the table, Maurice walked through to the bedroom, closed the door behind him and picked up some earplugs from the bedside table. The last thing he heard as he inserted the earplugs was a slight breeze that was gradually increasing in strength. He lay face down on the bed and immediately fell into a dream filled sleep. He didn't hear his front door swing open again as the breeze caught it.

Upstairs, Alan was removing the wizard outfit and going to bed too. He'd woken earlier on the sofa and had spent the intervening time glued to episodes of the Clangers on You tube. Alan, still intoxicated with the mushrooms, had decided that the Clangers were the best thing ever.
At last, Emmety Villa slept.

Doris yawned and then drove back to the campsite for a greatly needed sleep. She set her alarm for 9am. She was tired but could feel that Sunday was going to be a particularly important day and she didn't want to miss anything.

As Emmety Villa slept, the town was gradually beginning to wake up. The underappreciated council workmen quietly went about doing their usual magnificent job in clearing away the debris which had been left from the night before.

By 9am, the emmets could begin to trash the place all over again.

The cleaner from the Harbour Moon, Denzel's cousin Marcia, worked her way along the quay retrieving glasses which had been stolen from the pub and then abandoned. Why did people think that if they paid for the beer, it was okay to take the glass? The town was covered in items which had been stolen, beer towels, salt and pepper sellers, ashtrays and even a toilet brush. Marcia wondered if this just happened here or if visitors to Windsor Castle did the same thing? She spotted a fire extinguisher lying on its side between two parked cars. The inspection label on the side revealed it had come from the Grumpy. It had been discharged. Marcia struggled to understand the mentality of these people. She'd stick to cleaning as grim as it was. At least she didn't have to serve these people face to face.

A car pulled up beside her. Marcia quickly took in the tinted windows and huge tyres and the dealership sticker revealing the origin as Surrey. It looked like something her Uncle Cyril might use on his farm. Until today, this one had clearly never gone any further than an expensive chapel conversion to Waitrose in Walton on Thames.

The window went down with a smooth buzz and a man leaned across from the driver's side. "I say!" he announced himself loudly. Marcia looked around in case there was anyone else in the street "I'm talking to you" the man barked again and snapped his fingers twice at Marcia. "We've been driving all night. We want breakfast" he demanded.
"Oh you won't find anywhere open around here" Marcia answered. "The closest place to here that's open at this time of day is the Breakfast Hut"
"And where is this Breakfast Hut? " finger clicker barked again.
"It's right on the top of the hill by Caradon Mast" Marcia answered.

The man began jabbing at his Twat-nav as they were known locally. The window buzzed shut again and Desert Roamer pulled away.

Marcia smiled, it would be a long drive through the lanes in that thing, and the only breakfast he'd find on Caradon would be rocks and gorse. She hoped he was low on fuel.

"Bye then ass-hole" she raised a one fingered salute as he drove off.

On the main beach, Richard was also having an encounter with a visitor. Richard loved his home, but he struggled with visitors as much as Maurice did, he just didn't practice repelling them quite the same way.

Richard preferred avoidance and so he would get up early and try to remain as uncontaminated by contact as possible.

This morning he was walking along the sand parallel to the softly breaking waves. He was looking for sea glass. It was a beautiful peaceful morning, or at least it had been until a Mancunian accent interrupted his serenity. Richard had spotted the man emerging from a tent which had been pitched on the beach overnight. His worst fears were realised as the man began to address him.

"Olriiite mate, what are you looking for"
"Solitude" Richard answered icily.
Undeterred the man continued "I don't suppose you know what that white seagulls doing do you?"
Richard followed the man's pointing until his eyes rested on the bird he was being asked about.
"It's a Egret, pronounced Idiot!" Richard growled and then added "and there's no such thing as a seagull, the ones that live here are herring gulls"
"Oh, well, I never knew that" The visitor responded.
"Indeed. I would imagine that there's a great deal you don't know, like when to bugger off"
Richard left the open mouth tourist and stomped off.

Opposite the supermarket, the towns amused early birds stopped to photograph Dracula who was still asleep in the casket in the shop window.

Lowenna poured herself a forth mug of tea and

decided she would need the paracetamol her husband had offered her after all. She hadn't drunk that much for years. She wondered if Veryan was equally hung over. They should have gone for the universal hangover preventer she thought. It had been a long day; the kebab shop had been busy and she'd just wanted to get home. Next time she promised herself, the night was going to end with a large doner and chips.

She was still simmering that the panty pervert had had the audacity to target her garden.
It was Nana's party later but she still had a few hours to investigate. There was also the matter of Cousin Dave and his ID plus the location of the owner of the wallet she'd found.

She waited for the scenes of crimes team to arrive. Normally they wouldn't attend such an incident, but the frilly felon had stolen hundreds of pounds worth of underwear on her patch now. Lowenna didn't think he was dangerous, but he was certainly a little odd.

The forensic team happened to be just down the road. According to the CCTV, a pair in fancy dress had managed to lever the door off the little bakery at around 3am. They'd completely ignored the till and the little safe in the back room. However, they'd completely emptied the fridge, which had contained 160 precooked sausage rolls.

One of them had left a heavy black plastic gauntlet on the countertop. There was also a piece of silk cloth lying on the floor which had been identified as a cravat.

The burglary had been discovered by the owner when she'd realised the alarm which had been irritating her for an hour and a half was the one from her own shop.
Her husband wasn't back yet, he was probably still at the Old Goal. She wasn't worried, sometimes he could be gone for up to three days. She wondered if her boy, Derek, would be able to shed any light on who the masked men had been.

She'd looked through her husband's notebook and found the assistant chief constables' number. "No problem, I'll get someone right on it" He'd said when she'd rung him "We always

take care of our people" The ACC had assured
her. The Scenes of crime people had arrived
within half an hour.

Lowennas husband was just about to leave.
"Sorry love" he explained "I have to go, that prat
Denzel is still having trouble with the rats"
"I'm not surprised" Lowenna answered, "The
tight sod only gets his bins emptied once a
month. He gets his lackey to burn all the
cardboard in an incinerator down the Mill-pool. I
wonder if he's got a waste hauliers license?"

He kissed the top of his wife's head. "Why don't
you go back to bed for a bit?" He suggested
gently "There's nothing else you can do for
now"
"I will love" Lowenna answered "See you later,
go carefully eh?"
"I love you" he said softly as he slipped out
through the door.
"I love you too" Lowenna answered him.
She pushed the teapot to the far side of the
table and laid her head on her arm for a
snooze.

It was 7am when a silver car pulled up outside

Emmety Villa and pulled into one of the marked parking spaces. Kirsten used her apartment in the building as much as she could, but her work often kept her away. She noted the white van which was also parked in the private car park. Clearly that idiot Nigel from the house next door was taking liberties yet again she noted, she'd have to sort that out.

That was a job for later, right now she was hungry and delighted to be back in her favourite place. She was disappointed to see that the sleazy bloke from the bottom flat hadn't moved away yet. "I expect he's friends with Nigel" she told her dog as she reached into the back seat for an arm full of bags. "There's something really greasy about the pair of them" she continued talking the attentive fox terrier. "Come on then Jack, let's go up" She closed the car door and started to climb the steps. She spotted the ghastly plastic swan. "Oh god" she said to the dog "Some people eh?" Jack looked back knowingly and nipped over to the awful lawn ornament. "Oh good boy" Kirsten told him as he cocked a leg on Maurice's latest attempt at garden décor. He sniffed at the rubber balaclava Maurice had dropped earlier. Kirsten was too busy juggling her heavy load of bags to notice. For good measure, Jack scent marked the rubber head gear too.

As she passed Maurice's door, she noticed it swing on the breeze. For a horrible instant she thought the creepy neighbour might actually appear, and then the door swung back again. Jack went up the steps to sniff at the door. "No Jack" she instructed "You mustn't"
Jack nodded in acceptance and went back to join her on the way up to her own flat. He barked in excitement as she put her key in the lock. "Home at last Jack" she said brightly. Jack barked loudly again, and they went in.

River and Ocean were awake. They'd been woken first by unfamiliar row the seagulls the seagulls made and then they'd heard a dog barking downstairs. In the room next door, mummy and daddy were both snoring loudly. Both little girls were thirsty. The best cure for dehydration they'd learned from mummy, was more of the same. They were about to set off for the kitchen in search of cider when River spotted an enormous spider on the windowsill. "Don't hurt it" she told her sister pointing. Ocean took a step closer to investigate. "Ooo,

he's beautiful, shall we keep him?" she turned
to face her little sister.
"Yes, lets" River answered. Again, they moved
towards the door and then Ocean spotted
another similar arachnid on the curtains. She
pointed it out to River "Look, another one, it
must be his friend"

The two little girls looked all around the room.
In all they counted eight gigantic spiders. Any
other family would be halfway down the steps
by now, but not this one.
"How exciting" Ocean whispered, not wanting to
disturb the eight legged roommates.
Maurice would have been gravely disappointed
at their reaction.

Lowenna woke to a loud rapping on her door.
She smoothed down the front of her dressing
gown and opened it to find two men standing
there. She didn't recognise either of them and
for a moment thought she was about to be
introduced to their friend, the Lord Jesus Christ.

One of the men presumptuously began to move
as if he was going to walk straight in. "Scenes
of crime madam. We understand you've had an

incident" he announced. Lowenna stood firm.

"He was around the back; you can go that way" she jerked a thumb to indicate the side path. "You won't find much, just an imprint on the far side where he went over the bank"

The taller one tried to step inside again. The other man rolled his eyes. "Constable Cordon madam, we'll decide what's important here" he waved his identity card in Lowennas face "We'll need a statement from you. And we'd both get along a bit better once we've had a cup of tea" he indicated his colleague and then mimed a drinking motion. "Shall we go to the kitchen?" He tried again to step inside. The shorter one gave a small, dismayed shake of his head.

Lowenna was bristling like a hedgehog now. "No" she said firmly, "we shall not be going to the flaming kitchen" She'd had enough of this idiot already. She stepped back inside and slammed the door in his face.

Cordon knocked on the door again "Madam? Madam?" Lowenna decided it was time to get dressed.

By the time she'd showered and dressed properly, Cordon and his chum were waiting on the back doorstep unsure how to proceed. Clearly they'd had a look at the garden and from the landing window, Lowenna had seen the younger one take a measurement of the single indentation where Maurice had stepped up the bank.

She blocked the doorway firmly with her body and before they could speak demanded "Well then?"

Can we come inside madam? These things are much better discussed over a cup of tea." Cordon didn't give up easily

"Just tell me what you found" Lowenna barked irritably.

Cordon wasn't used to this approach. Usually the people he visited were traumatised.

Cordon loved feeling important and so despite the fact that most of the people he had to deal with were in shock, he liked to get them to bring him cups of tea and if he could wring a bacon sandwich out of anyone, he considered it a triumph.

"I really do think we ought to do this inside madam" he insisted Cordon was trying to look inside now. Lowenna changed her position just enough for Cordon to be able to see her three striped tunic hanging on the back of a kitchen chair.

"Oh" Cordon exclaimed "Are uniform already here then?"

"It's mine" Lowenna replied icily.

Cordon took and involuntary step back and went white. His silent colleague, who hated working with him, snorted as he stifled a laugh.

Lowenna turned sideways and pointed at the table. "SIT!" she commanded. Cordon and his smiling colleague did as they'd be instructed.

Lowenna deliberately slapped her palms on the table and leaned towards Cordon as she repeated her question "Well then?"

At that moment Cordon would have been less uncomfortable if he'd been confronted with Lucifer himself. He tried to draw back in his chair but there was nowhere to go.
His colleague was enjoying this immensely.

"W W We think he had size ten trainers on and he's about six feet tall and skinny" Cordon blurted out desperate now to leave.

"Oh I'm so glad they sent the premier squad" she answered sarcastically "I suppose you're giving away chocolate teapots along with your brilliant deductions too, now get out"

Cordon was on his feet in a flash. His colleague began to rise too. Lowenna turned to the quiet one "Not you love, would you like a cup of tea?"

She turned back to Cordon "Close the door quietly" she ordered his retreating back.

She went to fill the kettle and said in completely different demeanour "Well, constable moron introduced himself , what's your name love?"
"I'm so sorry about him" came the reply "I'm Rob, Rob Demellweek."

"And did you do your time in uniform in Plymouth Rob?"
"I did mam , lived there all my life"
"Oh good" Lowenna answered "perhaps you could have a look at this for me" She reached for the wallet she'd found the previous evening.

Camilla was trailing behind Monty. He wanted to re live a part of his youth and was insistent she come with him. He'd suggested she wear the tiger print leggings again, but Camilla had refused, they needed a wash. Now she was sporting a pair of fluorescent orange ones that were so tight Monty had unconsciously started humming the Camel Toe song.

The town clock struck seven times to announce the arrival of eight o clock.
It was far too early for Camilla, but the choice had been to stay in bed and Monty would have probably gotten amorous. Camilla's thoughts turned to the splendid examples of chavdom and her chat with Channella last night. She was feeling a little excited about later.

They found a cafe and Camilla plonked herself on a chair at an outside table while Monty went and ordered them breakfast. He was sweet she thought, and perhaps once her name was on the paperwork connected with his father's business, she would get the approval she'd spent her life seeking.

A loud female London accent behind her interrupted her train of thought She turned to glance at the source and realised with horror that she'd chosen to sit right next to Cowboy and his girlfriend. "and I want to see all you bank statements" the woman was saying. Camilla tried to make herself invisible. Monty came back with a tray loaded with coffees and croissants. There was something familiar about the man on the next table, but Monty couldn't place him. He smiled anyway "Morning" he offered brightly. Cowboy looked up and looked puzzled "Yeah mate" he answered and turned his attention back as the loud woman reeled off a list of financial instructions to him.

When Monty had sat down Cowboy leaned over to his girlfriend and asked her quietly "Oo the 'ell was that?"

Camilla let out a shriek as a gull swooped down

and stole her croissant. Monty reloaded the tray, and they went inside with their coffees. "Have mine" he indicated his plate.

"I didn't want a bloody croissant anyway" Camilla snapped back and rose to her feet. "I'm going to get myself a proper breakfast." A few minutes later she was sitting again. She looked happier now. She enthusiastically set about consuming a huge slice of lemon drizzle cake dressed in a generous portion of clotted cream. She'd also managed to acquire a small bottle of prosecco which she consumed with equal gusto.

With breakfast finished they continued the pursuit of Monty's memories. He'd assured Camilla they'd have a great time. Camilla really didn't understand how dragging poor little crabs out of the water and then leaving them to poach in a bucket on the quay would be fun. From what Monty had explained, you couldn't even eat them afterwards. Camilla watched enviously as a boatload of would be mackerel fishers chugged down the river heading seawards.

Monty spotted a sign outside a shop offering crabbing deals. There was a sign on a stand which informed them they could get bait inside. Monty selected the most expensive buckets and crab lines and picked up a net for each of them. They went in to pay.

"Where's a good place to catch crabs these days?" he asked the cheerful looking man behind the counter. The man smiled at him. "you might 'ave to wait a few days" he answered with a broad smile "disco dun open again until next weekend" he laughed loudly at his own joke and then continued "and anyway, what with all this waxing malarkey, I reckon most ov the abbitats bin destroyed these days. That's six pounds eighty thanks." he continued to chuckle at his own humour. Monty pretended not to notice. Camilla didn't have a clue what he was saying.
"Thas three-pound twenney change bouy" he handed the money to Monty and added "seriously, you wanna know the best place to get crabs? It's out of the buckets of the people crabbing next to you" He was still laughing as they left the shop.

Gradually the town began to come fully alive

again. Shopkeepers put their displays out trying to make sure the goods were within range of the sadly necessary cameras. The remaining cafes opened, and an assortment of catering and hospitality staff queued in the supermarket buying top ups for their masters. Other locals tried to get in and out of town before the emmets descended like the plague of ant's they'd been named after. Gulls took up sentry points ready for a busy day fishing for pasties and ice creams.

A pressing need to visit the toilet had finally woken Dracula and he'd risen to the delight of a greatly amused crowd which had gathered. Visitors and locals alike filmed the scene as he sat up in his coffin and raised an arm to protect his eyes from the glaring sunlight. He'd lurched like a drunk to escape into the much darker area at the back of the shop. As he vanished, they gave him a round of applause.

Lowenna was walking back towards the town now having been to visit Cousin Dave in his shed. He was delighted to be reunited with his cards and he confirmed he was also missing a large sum of cash. Like many of the notes in the town, the ones from Dave's wallet had Denzel's initials in pencil on them. Lowenna had left the notes with him too.

Rob Demellweek had recognised Troy immediately, any of his colleagues would have too. Troy and his Corsa were well known to all of them.
He was on his way back to Plymouth now and had volunteered to call in at Troy's mums house and find out what his movements were that weekend.

From what Lowenna had been able to deduce, Dave had lost his wallet in the social club and then his jacket had been stolen when he'd gone hunting for the wallet. Lowenna was on her way to the social club now. She knew there was bound to be someone there who could let her view the CCTV.
Dave had said he'd had his wages in his wallet plus another wad he'd been paid for a job he'd done for a mate, about £700 in all he reckoned.

Lowenna wondered where the rest of his money was now. As she walked along the quay a black Desert Roamer sped past her pulled up outside the pub on the harbour with an unnecessary squeal of brakes. A red-faced man jumped out from the driver's seat and hopped up the steps to the pub where he immediately began banging on the glass with a fist. "I want a word with you!" he bellowed.

Lowenna was casually dressed, she wasn't supposed to be on duty. She fished her ID from her handbag and went to see what all the fuss was about.
As she approached the vehicle, a marked squad car turned onto the quay road. She put up her hand to flag it down. The driver recognised the Sargent instantly and stopped beside her.

"What's going on this morning then?" she asked the driver.

"We had a report of a bloke in a Desert roamer trying to break into the tool store up Caradon" he told her "And half a dozen reports of the same bloke driving dangerously in the lanes" Lowenna pointed at the Roamer driver who was utterly oblivious to the presence of the police car. "I think he's your one, do you want me to stick around?"

Everyone in the station knew of Lowennas
Aikido prowess but Mark could see she was
supposed to be off duty. "It's fine thanks Mam,
me and Terry will get it sorted."

"Have fun" Lowenna smiled ironically.

River and Ocean were disappointed not to find
any cider in the fridge. Mummy and Daddy
were still asleep, so they breakfasted on fizzy
pop and chocolate biscuits, it was just like
being at home. They'd tried to turn the
television on but it was lifeless.

"Let's have a look outside" Ocean suggested.

Still in their pyjamas, the two little girls left the
door of the apartment ajar and taking the
biscuits with them, set off down the stairs.
Jack barked as they passed his door. He
pressed his nose up to the glass. The girls
waved to him.

Once outside it wasn't very long before they
spotted Maurice's front door swinging in the
breeze. "Let's go inside" River urged her sister.
Ocean was feeling a little more cautious and so

they walked up to the windows and had a good look inside. There was no one there. They ran back around to the door and ventured in. From behind the closed bedroom door, they could hear Maurice snoring loudly. They giggled. "It sounds just like mummy" Ocean told her little sister "What's in here?" she pushed the kitchen door gently.

Denzel's open briefcase was the only thing in the room that they noticed.
Their mouths fell open.

Ocean knew better than to waste time at a moment like this. She stepped forward, took a bundle of twenties in each hand and urged her little sister "We must be really quick!" She darted towards the door and made her exit. River followed her sister and reached up to the case. It was just out of reach, so she pulled one of the kitchen chairs towards the table and clambered up. Just as Ocean had done, she grabbed a bundle of twenties in each hand and then quickly departed the scene to follow her sister back up the stairs and into their holiday apartment. She completely forgot about the half packet of chocolate biscuits she'd left on

Maurice's table. She slammed the door of the apartment behind her and went to the room she was sharing with her sister. They put their bundles on one of the beds. "We ought to hide this" Ocean said. River nodded in agreement. She picked up her unicorn satchel and they set about concealing the money.

In the social club, Lowenna replayed the footage of Leafetta and Troy from the day before. The angle of the camera in the foyer wasn't great, but after Dave had stumbled outside, Leafetta had raised her hand to clearly show a wallet. What on earth was the girl wearing?

Lowenna thought the couple wouldn't have had the brains to go very far, she rummaged in her bag and rang Veryan.

Veryan answered groggily. "Are you busy love?" Lowenna asked her "I know you're off duty, but it's work related, and our Dave's had his wallet nicked again"

Veryan snapped into wakefulness. Poor Dave, he had such a history of bad luck, mostly lager related but bad luck, nevertheless. Everybody liked Dave.

"I can be down in about three quarters of an hour" she told her cousin "Have you had breakfast?" Lowenna had drunk plenty of tea but she was rumbling now. They agreed to meet in the cafe on the seafront.

Camilla was enjoying herself far more than she'd expected. They'd chosen a spot on the quay and although there was a small trickle of traffic coming along the road behind them, they'd managed to find a place where the sun shone brightly. Most importantly, Camilla was catching more crabs then Monty.

A youth on an unnecessarily load motorbike revved the engine to impress a couple of his mates a few yards away.

Camilla stood to drop another captive into her bucket and tugged at her leggings to adjust them.

"Itchyfanni" a voice said behind her. She turned swiftly on the man, but he clearly wasn't looking at her. He was pointing out the motorbike to his son "You can always tell the Japanese one's by the noise son"

Just around the corner, Doris headed for the
only remaining vacant table outside the
seafront cafe. A pleasant young woman had
stepped past her with a cheery "Good morning"
and had joined a slightly older woman who was
just putting her phone down.

Coppers thought Doris and smiled. She
wondered if she'd been that apparent back in
her days in Bristol. Over time and a very odd
workshop on Dartmoor, she'd learned how to
blend with her surroundings and become
virtually invisible, even when in the middle of a
group of people. Her instructor on the
'Becoming the fox' weekend had taught her a
lot about urban camouflage, you always
recognised your own type though, and they
always recognised you.

Lowenna had already made her assessment of
Doris as she'd been looking for a table.
Probably on holiday but defiantly a fellow police
officer. Now as Doris took a seat next to Veryan
and Lowenna, Lowenna knew that though she
had to talk in guarded terms, it wouldn't matter

if the newcomer overheard a little. A young man
came to take their order and then stopped
beside Doris to repeat the process.

Lowenna explained about the wallet to Veryan.
"Bless him, he was still asleep when I got there"
she said "Honking like a brewery, he must have
put some away yesterday"
Veryan nodded sympathetically "Poor Dave.
Mind you, if I was married to Jessica I'd drink
like that too"

Lowenna continued "I just got off the phone to
one of the Plymouth lads and he's given me an
accommodation address for this little scroat.
"She handed Veryan the wallet "Apparently he's
up at Emmety Villa"

On the table next door Doris's ears pricked up.
She'd been just about to bite into her sausage,
now it hovered in front of her mouth, wobbling a
little on the fork.
Lowenna took another bite of her toast.
"I also had an early morning visit"
Veryan gasped as she knew instantly that
Lowenna was referring to the panty pilferer .
"Oh my god" she put down her coffee cup "what

happened?"

Lowenna told the tale. Trying to be as discreet as possible, Doris eavesdropped chewing slowly. When Lowenna mentioned the rubber balaclava, Doris nearly spat out her sausage.

Back at Seaview, Alan was having breakfast too. He'd been woken by what sounded like a brontosaurus clumping around in the holiday apartment upstairs. There was a loud thud and inside the dry lined walls, Alan could hear plaster dust falling down.

Upstairs, River and Ocean had retreated to their bedroom and were bouncing off the mattresses onto the floor. They had been trampolining on the sofa, but all the springiness had quickly disappeared. There was another loud thump, Alan cringed again. He wasn't feeling great and Eileen would be home soon. He rose to open the kitchen window and let some air in. Someone was having a bonfire he thought, and then watched a cloud of dense smoke drift past his window.

"Bloody Hell!" for an instant he thought the building was on fire, and then he spotted the grubby looking visitor from the holiday apartment downstairs. He was inhaling from something that looked like a majorette's kazoo. Alan decided to sit down again.

It was only then that the full horror of last night's revelation came back to him.
Maurice was the grand master. Alan put his hands over his face. After all that effort, and now he'd made himself subject to Alan's authority. "Oh god" he appealed and began gently rocking. Upstairs there were new noises as Damien and Channella joined the world of the conscious.

"This bloody water still int working" Channella shouted from the bathroom. "And where the hell did all these flies come from?"

"Are we going on the glass bottom boat today?" River asked her father.

"Yes darling, we will, but we'll have a look around the shops first eh?"
River was pleased and nudged her big sister with a smile. A look around the shops for their family meant an expedition where no money was going to change hands, that didn't mean

they'd come home without a few souvenirs though. She quite fancied having another go at that blue ice cream too.

Elsewhere in the building, Kirsten and Jack had finished breakfast. Jack was particularly excited. Originally, he'd been trained as a sniffer dog for Southampton Customs.
He was great at finding drugs, but he just couldn't contain himself. The drill was supposed to be that when he detected something illicit, he sat quietly and raised a paw to indicate to his handler there was something to investigate further. In practice he would do this, and then in his doggy fashion, attempt to befriend the suspect. It had all been a little unprofessional.

Jack was so used to getting treats for finding contraband that he would go through his routine whether he found a kilo of heroin or a packet of indigestion tablets. Jack had retired early. Despite that, he still had a keen nose and he'd never forgotten his training.
The smoke drifting up from Troy had him practically beside himself with excitement. In Jacks head, he was about to earn a lot of extra biscuits.

Denzel had returned to the yellow Jaguar and snatched a parking ticket off the windscreen. He'd been illegally parked, where he usually did, on the road outside one of his chip shops. He screwed up the ticket and threw it down onto the road. Didn't they know who he was? How dare they! Denzel would see to it that whoever had written the ticket would be looking for a new job by Monday morning.

The ticket, on top of his most recent conversation, had left him incandescent. Katrina had beaten him too it. She'd handed him her notice and although the rent was paid up front for the next two months, she was moving out of the flat today. Denzel wasn't going to be sacking anyone. "I'm going to work for Trevor the Turbot" she'd explained. "And he's asked me to look after his house until he comes back from Portugal"

Trevor owned a shop on the edge of town and a chip van on one of the campsites.
He was Denzel's only rival in the fish and chip business, and the two had been enemies ever since their school days. Trevor wasn't related to

Denzel, and he wasn't a member of the special club. Denzel desperately wanted to hound Trevor out of the town, but Trevor had connections too. Denzel was livid. As he pulled out without looking, he caught the back wheel of a motorbike which had been making circuits of the seafront, spilling the rider into a parking bay. The bike lay in the road with the back wheel still spinning. Denzel didn't notice a thing as he sped off.

The rider lay in the road groaning and clutching his groin

"My poor Itchyfanni, my poor poor Itchyfanni"

Lowenna and Veryan had watched with delight as the ticket had been placed on Denzel's windscreen. They'd loitered for a few minutes wanting to see his face when he came out of his shop. He might well be a cousin, but neither of them was under any illusions about what Denzel was.

They watched in horror as the youth was knocked off his bike and now, they rushed over to help him.

Doris had been watching too. The ghastly Jaguar was the same one which had stopped at

Maurice's lair last night. She made a note on her phone and continued on her way. Maurice would probably be up again soon, and with the information she'd just learned, she was pretty certain things were about to take a turn in the right direction. On her way up the quay she'd noticed a couple crabbing. Monty was facing the water. Doris was too dazzled by Camilla's leggings to notice Monty "Oh my god" she'd muttered under her breath as she'd walked past shaking her head in disbelief.

Lowenna called one of her colleagues while Veryan called an ambulance. They waited until both had arrived and then set off to visit Troy at Emmety Villa

Doris was already a good way along the quay, towards Emmety Villa

Denzel was going to get his briefcase back, and was heading towards Emmety Villa too.

At Emmety Villa, Alan was feeling sorry for himself.

Troy was stoned.

Damien and Channella were trying to wash.

And River and Ocean were full of fizzy pop and chocolate biscuits. They
were very excited, as was Jack.

In his kitchen, Maurice was looking at half a packet of chocolate biscuits and wondering where the hell it had appeared from.

Troy and Leafetta joined Channella and Damien upstairs.

Leafetta watched River picking her nose. "Your kids are so cute, you're great parents," she told them as she passed a joint to Channella. She continued "Me and Troy want to start a family don't we lover?"

Damien saw an opportunity here. "How would you like to have them for company for the afternoon?"

Troy wasn't keen, especially as he was still nursing the bruises he acquired the night before. On the other hand, if they had the giwls with them, Leafetta wouldn't be able to make any intimate demands on him. For the first time since he was 14, he really wasn't in the mood. She'd done her best to coax him when she'd returned that morning, and then she'd seen the bruises.

She kept forgetting, and Leafetta had needs, that was one of the things Troy liked about her. Troy looked at the giwls with fresh eyes now. The arcades, the beach, perhaps a walk around the shops "Yes we'd love to" he answered enthusiastically. Leafetta was delighted.

Channella went on to extol her offspring's talent when it came to procurement. Damien finished by adding, "We just fancy a quiet afternoon in don't we hun?" he put his clasped hands to his face in a classic sleep gesture.

Channella looked at Damien appreciatively; he'd just cleared the way for their afternoon with Monty and Camilla.

In the town, Denzel had decided that rather than drive through the hordes of people, he'd take an alternative route. He was now stuck on a hill behind a camper van which was firmly stuck between two buildings where the road narrowed.

The sign at the top had warned motorists of the restrictions. Like many before him, the driver of the camper van had ignored the warning and trusted his Sat Nav. It would take a tractor to extricate the mangled camper now.

Denzel would have reversed but there were at least six cars behind him. The one at the back didn't seem to be aware he had a reverse gear. Denzel's mood wasn't getting any better. "Bleedy tossin spanners" he cursed. He flicked on the CD player, One Frankie goes to Hollywood track ended and the opening notes of 'The power of love' filled the air. In between continuing to swear at the visitors, he sang along.

Monty was finally sated; it was probably something to do with the fact that he had eight crabs and Camilla had hoisted up over thirty. They tipped the little green captives back into the water and walked off, abandoning the lines, nets and buckets on the quay along with their other rubbish.

Camilla rang Channella for directions.

Doris had arrived at Emmety Villa. On an earlier visit to the building, she'd spotted the visitors patio. Being careful not to let herself be seen; she entered the garden of the house next door. She'd talked to the owner earlier in the week. A nice woman, she'd told Doris that on Sunday she always had the carvery in the Smugglers, as did most of the locals. It was the best for miles she'd said. Doris took a chance, if the nice lady was home, she'd say she was trying to remember the name of the restaurant.

She began climbing the steps. She'd been lucky, there was no one there. Doris stepped off the path, nipped across the lawn and then hopped over the wall onto the visitor patio. From here she could listen to what was going on at Maurice's flat without being seen. She could also watch the steps.

Next to arrive were Lowenna and Veryan. They headed straight for the door of the lower flat.

Lowenna pointed at the ghastly plastic swan. "Honestly, some people eh?" They were almost at the top of the steps when Veryan spotted something black lying on the ground next to the swan.

"Psst"" she nudged Lowenna with a finger to her lips. With her other hand she pointed "Look!"

"Oh my god" Lowennas eyes widened as she realised what she was looking at.

"Quick" She told Veryan "Back down"

At the bottom of the steps they positioned themselves behind the same hedge Doris had been using to conceal herself earlier.

"Do you think he lives in there?" Veryan asked.

"I don't know, but I'm going to call the boys up and get them over here before we go in"

Lowenna took out her phone and began dialling her on duty colleagues.

In Emmety Villa, everything had been arranged. River and Ocean had happily agreed to go with

Troy and Leafetta. Mummy and Daddy didn't have many rules, but they could do practically anything they wanted with these two. River went into the bedroom to collect her satchel. Channella intervened. "you don't need that poppet, why don't you leave it here" River shook her head. Channella knew how to play this "You might find a new one while you're out, then you'll have to carry two" River thought about it.

"Oh okay" she said and dropped her bag. It hit the floor with a thunk.

"What on earth have you got in there?" it dawned on Channella there might be something of value "have you got another lifeboat?" she smiled.

River shook her head. Ocean picked up the bag and began to head back towards the bedroom with it. Channella stepped in "Just a minute, let me see" Ocean shook her head now. Damien plucked the bag from his daughters' grasp.

"Let's have a look shall we?" he tugged open the zipper and tipped the contents of the bag onto the floor.

Four adults inhaled sharply.

Maurice counted the money again; it was £8'000 light. "That bloody Denzel" he kept mumbling, and then his gaze fell back on the biscuits.

He'd been so focused on the money he hadn't noticed his door. It swung on the breeze again. Maurice leapt to his feet as he heard the hinges squeak. Someone had been in his flat. "The thieving bastards!" he shouted.

Outside on the visitor's patio, Doris heard Maurice's exclamation. She peeped at the steps to see if he was outside.

She could barely believe her eyes when she saw the woman with the orange leggings walking up them, and right behind her, the other man Doris had been trying to find for so long, Montague Chalmers.

Inside his apartment, Alan had decided the only way he could settle his stomach was a hair of the dog. The only thing he had was a bottle of Crème de menthe. He took a generous swig from the bottle.

No sooner had Monty and Camilla begun to climb the steps than Lowennas phone buzzed. "We're just sorting out an incident in town" one of the PC's told her
"Mark and Pete were taking their break so I've asked them to come up, they're walking, be with you asap, got to go, we're almost done."

Lowenna glanced down the road. The station was only a couple of hundred yards from here. She could see Mark and Peter now. She waited for a few minutes and then quickly briefed them when they arrived.

"No one is to leave until we've spoken to everyone. Ronnie and Reginald will be here when they finish in town"

They began climbing the steps.

Denzel was free of the traffic blockage. Tony had come from the seafront in the tractor he used to maintain the beach. The camper van was only fit for scrap now, but Denzel cared nothing about that. He was going to collect his briefcase, and then he was going to find someone else to sack.

"Where did you get it?" Channella demanded. She didn't mind the giwls taking things, but this amount of money was going to have serious repercussions.

"Erm, perhaps it would be better if we left? We can do something tomorrow if you like?" Leafetta was bright enough to know when to haul her considerable acreage of lycred ass.

Downstairs Lowenna paused.

"Stay here by the front doors" Lowenna picked up the rubber balaclava gingerly with a stick.

"It must be him" she said to Veryan.

There were voices as Monty and Camilla passed the young couple from Plymouth on the stairs inside.
Lowenna and her team stepped through the front door just as Troy and Leafetta appeared.

Troy still had a smoking joint in his hand.

"Arrest them both Lowenna" instructed Mark, and then seeing Leafetta and Troy crumple into submission indicated the door of their apartment and added "let's go inside."

Denzel stopped his car in the road not bothering with the normal niceties of parking. He was Denzel Sprygelly and Denzel could bloody well do what Denzel Sprygelly bloody well wanted. He'd lived in the town all his life , he had special privileges.
He slammed the yellow door.

The CD player continued to play Burt Bacharach

"What the world, needs now, is love, sweet love"

He stomped up the steps blissfully unaware of the presence of the four police officers already inside.

Maurice's door was open. Denzel knocked loudly and called "It's Denzel." He walked in.

Maurice recognised there was about to be a problem and was instantly defensive.

Before Denzel could say another word Maurice went on the attack. "It's short!" He shouted at Denzel.

Maurice had no idea what had happened while he slept, but that was irrelevant. They'd agreed a price and Denzel; loaded, wealthy, dishonest Denzel, was going to have to make up the shortfall.

"It bleedy wasn't, I counted it myself" Denzel snapped back.

The argument was underway. .

On the other side of the building, Kirsten opened her front door and Jack was off before she could stop him. He shot down the side of the lawn and into the hallway. He stopped to bark at the door of Troy and Leafettas apartment and then caught another enticing scent. He shot up the stairs in pursuit of Camilla and the contents of her handbag.
He was just too late. As he reached the door,

Monty had closed it behind him. Jack began barking with enthusiasm.

Doris could hear Maurice and Denzel arguing.

Now was the time to show herself she decided.

As she moved away from the visitors patio and around the corner of the building into the main garden, another two coppers in uniform arrived
.

Hearing the cuffufle, they began to hurriedly climb the steps.
"Call for back up" Ronnie panted to Reggie.

Maurice, oblivious to the other scenes evolving in the building ,heard footsteps and glanced out of the window. He almost lost his voice for a second as he spotted the uniforms coming up the steps .

The flat was full of stolen underwear, it was on the radiators and on clothes horses., it was on display in every room in the flat.
There was far too much to hide it all in time.

"You bletherin bloody idiot" he shouted at Denzel, "You've bloody well led 'em right to us" Maurice raised a finger and pointed as he shouted "Shut the bloody door!"

Denzel, not understanding but still angry from earlier, turned and slammed the door before turning his attention back on Maurice.

"I always knew you were a spannering wanker!" he spat "You're just like all the other emmets" he growled venomously.

Maurice picked up the biscuits and threw them at Denzel.

Lowenna and Veryan watched as Troy and Leafetta were handcuffed. "Veryan love" Lowenna said "Go and see what all that barking is about will you?"

Veryan almost collided with Kirsten who was in hot pursuit of Jack. Thinking Veryan was a holiday maker she quickly explained "I'm really sorry, he's an ex drugs dog and sometimes he just takes off"

Jack was still barking and scratching at the upstairs door. It was going to be many biscuit time for Jacky boy. He allowed himself a doggy smile. He knew he'd done well. His tail was wagging ecstatically.

Veryan caught on quickly. She poked her head back inside the flat and asked Lowenna "Can one of the chaps come with me? I think we've got another situation upstairs"

The two uniformed officers outside were panting as they reached the top of the steps. Before they could go any further, they were intercepted by Doris. "He's in there" she told them pointing at Maurice's door. The new arrivals had no idea who Doris was, but they responded to the authority in her voice. Ronald began pounding on the door as the shouting inside continued.

"Police! Open up!"

"I'm the master here now!" There was a loud crash as Denzel lurched towards Maurice with a clenched fist. Maurice darted around the table and thrust a chair towards Denzel sending him careering to the floor.

As he tried to pull himself up, Denzel spotted a bright green pair of apple catchers hanging on the radiator. He'd have recognised them anywhere. They were his sisters.

"You're pathetic" Denzel hollered as he tried to get back to his feet "And your rubber gear is nothing but cheap recycled bicycle tyres. You can still see the tread"

It was the ultimate fetish fanciers insult.

Maurice was enraged.

"You're nothing but a pasty fiddler" Maurice retorted as he snatched the toaster from the side and hurled it at the prostrate figure. The toaster caught by the plug and recoiled hitting Maurice square in the chest.

"You can't even steal decent underwear" Denzel yelled mocking Maurice as he clambered to his feet. His eyes desperately searched for something to throw back. He snatched a framed wedding photograph from the dresser.

Maurice lifted a hand in a stop gesture "No please, not that" he pleaded.

Denzel let the photograph drop and hurled a teapot instead, narrowly missing Maurice's head.

Lowenna was outside Maurice's door too now. She lifted a well-trained leg, and booted the door hard. There was a satisfying crash as the wood splintered and the door sprung open.

She let Ronnie and Reginald dive past her and followed them in.

Upstairs in his flat, Alan , hearing the sudden explosion of noises, took another swig from the bottle "I just want peace and quiet" he whimpered.

As her colleagues restrained Denzel and Maurice, Lowenna tried to take everything in.

There was a briefcase full of money. As she peered closer, she could read the name plaque his mother had so lovingly had inscribed. Denzel Olivier Sprygelly.

As Maurice and Denzel were introduced to the cold embrace of handcuffs, Maurice allowed a pleasured sigh to escape. Everyone in the room, including Denzel, looked disgusted.

There was underwear everywhere. Hanging from the pocket of Maurice's dressing gown was something black and familiar. Lowenna reached forward and plucked them out.

"I believe these belong to me"

"You'll never prove anything" sneered Maurice "Everything here is circumstantial, you haven't got proof of anything"

"Explain this then" Lowenna was still holding the stick with the rubber balaclava. She stepped forward and raised it in front of Maurice's face.

"That's my personal property" Maurice blustered "And I have lots of friends who have identical ones" He tried to escape the strong restraining hands that held him in a bid to grab his rubber wear. He fell over.

Unseen by anyone, Doris had also entered the flat. "Oh yes she can prove something Chief Inspector." She paused for a second "or should I say, former Chief Inspector" and then in a voice loaded with satisfaction she held up her special camera and waved it at Maurice "It's all here".

Doris stopped and gawped as she looked around the room at all the underwear.

"Oh my god Maurice, you just don't know when to stop"

Lowenna turned to Doris "Erm, sorry love, but who are you?"

Doris looked at Lowenna. "I'm his wife, Doris Thomas, and I can tell you all about him"
She quickly added "There's someone else here you need to arrest too"

Upstairs, Veryan and Peter ordered everyone in the top flat to sit down. Jack was wiggling

excitedly as he pawed at Camilla's handbag.
The room was still full of smoke from the joints
Troy had been passing around.
The bundles of twenties were still in full view on
the floor.
Damien looked to Channella for help. She
shrugged her shoulders.
Monty was trying to escape. "What ever
happened here is nothing to do with us" He
tried to take Camilla's arm and lever her
towards the door.
"I think you need to sit down" Veryan ordered
him. He sat down meekly as the heavy
footsteps of more reinforcements clattered on
the stairway.

Veryan and Lowenna walked down the steps of
Emmety Villa. Doris followed them.

Troy and Leafetta had been arrested. The
CCTV from the social club would be enough
evidence to sort them out.

Maurice and Denzel had been arrested and had
a lot of explaining to do.

Monty had been arrested for fraud and thanks to Jack, Camilla had been arrested for possession of unlicensed pharmaceuticals.

Channella and Damien had been invited to the station to answer some questions about how they'd come into the possession of £8'000 and also about several incidents involving two little girls, remarkably like their daughters.

"Let's go for a drink and have a chat" Lowenna suggested to Veryan and Doris.

Inside his flat, Alan had finished the bottle. He was hugging himself and rocking. He'd put his outfit from the night before back on. "I just want to be a wizard" he kept repeating tearfully. He didn't want to be a special club member anymore.
He looked over at the kitchen corner to where he'd dumped his new briefcase and new apron into a black bin liner.

Epilogue.

Uncle Keith had been delighted to be released. There wasn't enough room in the cells for all the newcomers. When he'd woken in the tiny room. He had no idea why he was there, so he'd refused to say a word. He was charged with indecent exposure and shown the door.

"Thank god it was only that" he kept telling himself. For a few horrible hours he thought his scams had been discovered. Oh well, best to keep looking forward.
He took his phone from pocket. "Cowboy. I think I've got us another little job"

Printed in Great Britain
by Amazon

49230714R00160